Falling INTO THE BLACK

Falling
INTO THE BLACK

LAUREN RUNOW

Beta read and edited by Indie Solutions, www.murphyrae.net.

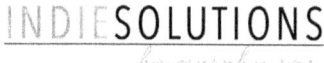

Cover Images © Adobe Stock – Andriy Petrenko
Back cover photo taken by Ryan Bates Photography
Cover Design © Designed With Grace

For Stefanie Pace
Thank you for all you do!

Books by
LAUREN RUNOW

Unwritten
Rewritten

Black Widow

The High Road (novella)

Gravity

Falling Into The Black

Chapter 1

EVANGELINE

I can't take my eyes off the photo staring back at me. Instead of closing my computer for the day, I decided to take one quick glance at Facebook before heading out for the night. Now I'm regretting that choice—big time.

So many memories, so many lies, so many nights spent crying myself to sleep, yet here I am, years later, brought back to my nightmare with one click of a mouse.

Actually, it was one careless friend request.

I left that world behind me, never to look back. Changing everything about me, including my name, and moving to San Francisco.

I guess I didn't try to hide hard enough.

There's always that one person who's known you for so long that they know everything about you, including the fact you went by your stepfather's last name instead of your real father's, who passed away right after you were born. My mother changed it when she remarried so we'd have the same last name.

This friend also knew I hated my real name when I was younger. Back then I wanted to shorten it to Angie, but my mom wouldn't let me. The older I got, the more I grew to appreciate the uniqueness of my name, and I thanked her then for not allowing me to change it.

How ironic I end up changing it anyway, just for other reasons now, and I'll admit, I miss Evangeline.

So yeah, leave it to this childhood friend to find me.

When I saw Kaitlyn's name pop up under the friend request tab, an instant smile touched my lips, and I clicked accept before I thought about what I was really doing. She sent me a message after that, asking if it really was me. I said yes, wrote a little more but then never responded to her again. She's from my past, and not someone I want in my present.

Now I'm kicking myself for that one mindless second from two weeks ago. I thought since we didn't have any friends in common it would be okay. I didn't take *this* into consideration.

Ten sets of eyes are looking back at me from her #TBT picture, sending my stomach into a tailspin.

It's the two sets not looking back that are pushing me over the edge.

No, those are looking only at each other for what would be the last time.

Against my better judgment, I click on the image I'm tagged in, torturing myself that much more. I know I should just remove my name from the photo, go back to my little corner of the world, away from everyone else, but I can't.

Instead, I click on the comments, noticing he's identified in the photo as well, and he's left a comment. Before I read it, I close my eyes tightly, fighting the tears threatening to spill over then close the window completely.

I can't go there.

I haven't told my boss, Kamii Schafer, or anyone for that matter, but I've worked for this law firm long enough, and I've decided to take my first step toward obtaining my law degree.

Kamii's this amazing attorney and has been encouraging me to go back to school for a while now. So, I finally decided to enroll in a night class, Intro to Law, just to see how I do before I jump in with both feet.

My class will be on Mondays, Wednesdays, and Fridays from six to nine at night. With a quick glance at my watch, I grab my bag and head off to a new beginning, trying to forget my past.

Standing outside the big wooden doors of an old church converted into a lecture hall, I realize this is it. I wrap my fingers tightly around the strap of my bag, take a deep breath, and then open the door…hopefully, one to a new life for me.

I walk inside and am struck by how much the space still looks like a church. Rows of wooden pews line the space with an altar at the top, now hosting a desk and freestanding whiteboard. Large, stained-glass windows with images of doves and children accent the room with the setting sun, glistening through the vibrant colors.

My class is in a large room off the main auditorium that must have been the original dining hall. When I walk in, I notice only a third of the seats are occupied by students, who sit scattered throughout the room. Instead of interacting, everyone is looking down, giving their attention to whatever device they have in front of them like they're hoping no one will approach them.

I'm a talkative, outgoing person, so the sight is an instant turnoff. I try to ignore it as I walk down the aisle and sit in the front row, exactly where everyone seems to be avoiding the most.

With my head held high, not buried in an electronic device, my attention is brought to the front when I catch the eye of a man walking in, which I assume is my new professor.

I'm not sure why I expected an old man with his shirt half tucked in and a crooked bowtie, but that is certainly not what I got. There's nothing about this man that screams professor.

The exact opposite, actually.

The way his broad shoulders stand out over his fit figure accentuate his build but not in a muscular kind of way. Instantly, my mind wonders what his arms would feel like wrapped around me.

I quickly glance down at my class schedule to see the name C. Spence listed as the professor. Thoughts on what the C stands for rush through my brain. He looks more like someone who rowed for the crew team rather than someone who played football, so I don't picture him being Charlie, Chris or anything more traditional like that. The way his thin, dark frame glasses sit perfectly on his face give him this indie, cool-guy look, so he could be a Conner or Christian.

There's something unique about the way he walks into the room with his dark eyes taking in every face as he strolls up to the desk. He doesn't carry a briefcase or side satchel. Instead, he props his black backpack up with a huge Vans patch stitched to the top of it.

I bite my lower lip. He's definitely an unexpected surprise, and if we were in any other situation, I'd be making it a point to go home with him tonight.

He places two hands on the desk and looks out into the audience. Starting at the far back, he studies every single person in the room like he's trying to read them, chapter by chapter, deciding what this class' book is all about. It's not until the very end that his eyes reach mine, and I swear I see a slight pull to his lips before he turns around to write something on the board.

I check out his lean arm as he moves swiftly across the white wall spelling out *How well can you read people?* before turning around and clearing his throat to get everyone's attention.

He doesn't say hello or introduce himself. He simply states, "Let's play a game, shall we?"

Every student looks around, silently questioning their teacher's words.

No one responds, so he continues, "I have here a class list with everyone's name on it. I bet I can guess each of your names by matching them to this list."

I hear a few laughs from people under their breaths until one student speaks up. "That's impossible."

"Really? Why do you say that?" he responds with a tilt to his head as he slowly approaches the student sitting about ten rows back and to the right of me.

After only taking a few steps forward, seemingly to get a better look, he turns around and walks back to his desk.

My eyes instantly roam the full length of his body as he leans back against the edge of the desk and crosses his left leg over his right while his arms are folded in front of his body.

The dark jeans he has on tug in all the right places, and I'd be a fool not to notice the bulge staring me in the face. When my eyes move up his torso and further to his jaw, I notice he's staring directly at me. Only this time, the smirk stays on his face before he turns his attention back to the student.

"There's got to be fifty students in the class. That's statistically impossible," the male student adds.

"So, then tell me, Adam, how did I know that was you?"

The student laughs is disbelief. "No way."

"I'm right, aren't I?"

"Okay, I'll give you that. How did you know my name?"

"Because I did my research, I paid attention, and in the end, I crossed my fingers and hoped for the best."

The other students laugh before another female sits up in her chair. "Okay, me next."

He studies her slightly, turning to grab his class list before looking down and up at her again. "Tell me first, why do you want to be a lawyer?"

"Because I want to help those who truly need me and put the bastards who deserve to be locked away there for good."

"Ah, you're Kelli." He snaps his finger before pointing it at her.

She lets out a little yelp in surprise. "How did you do that? How did my answer get you there?"

"It wasn't your answer. It was your voice, or more importantly, your accent. You see, I did research on every single one of you. I searched out your social media accounts—which by the way, some of you"—he stops and shakes his head in a questionable manner, sucking in a breath—"should really be careful about what you put out there. I'm shocked, to say the least." That gets another laugh out of everyone. "All, but a very slim few of you, I was able to access your accounts, obtain your whereabouts, who you went to school with, who you hung out with, and more importantly, where you grew up. Your accent, my dear, gave you away. Clearly from Chicago. That instantly told me you were Kelli."

"If you accessed our social media accounts then you saw our pictures, too, so you aren't that sneaky," another student argues.

Professor Spence nods his head. "Ah, yes, very true, but yet you see, not everyone's profile is set up the same. Some had privacy settings, so I couldn't access your photos, only the ones you were tagged in. So if I'm looking at a picture of five females, it's hard to say which one is you. I had to narrow down the options, learn as much as I could, and then in the end"—he pauses for dramatic effect—"take a gamble and hope like shit I'm right."

The class laughs again, and I love that our teacher is freaking badass. Yes, it's been years since I sat in a classroom, and I've never taken a college course, so maybe this is just the way things are done, but so far, I think I'm going to like this class.

"So keep going, see if you can name us all," a guy from two rows back shouts.

"Okay, stand up," he says. "And…" He looks around the room as if he's searching for someone in particular. "You, all the way in the back, stand up and walk down here. Grab your stuff too, come down and join us, stay awhile," he jokes.

The way he talks so nonchalantly as he strolls back to his desk with a grin on his face, looking at his class list and pulling out another notepad from his backpack, makes my heart rate beat just a little faster. And yes, I totally took a sneak peek at his ass, because, um, why not?

When he turns back around, both of the male students are standing next to each other. I study their appearance, and I can tell why he chose them. They do resemble each other physically, but they're uniquely different in their own ways.

"I'm here, so what's my name?" the guy who had to come closer asks.

Professor Spence studies them before saying, "You're Alex, and you're Paul." He points to each one as he identifies them.

They both look at each other and smirk, nodding their heads in agreement. Alex looks down at what he's wearing, asking, "What gave it away?"

"You're wearing flip-flops. I saw that you, Alex, are from San Diego, and you, Paul, are from Texas. Look, Paul's jeans are tighter than your baggy jeans, so I looked for subtle clues. It's not always what you know; it's the little things you don't know that help solve the problem."

"So that's the purpose of this little game?" I question. "Looking for things that others wouldn't normally notice?"

"Well then, someone's catching on, Ashley."

My lips curl into what I hope is the most mischievous smile, trying to tell him he's right before I nail him dead-on. The group talks amongst themselves in surprise again, and he goes to walk back to the board before I stop him. "Wrong."

Gasps of disbelief fill the classroom.

He drops his head, and I watch as his shoulders give away the laugh he's hiding. "You don't always win when you gamble, now, do you?"

"No, you don't." I bite back a grin.

He turns around and looks back down at his class list. His eyes twinkle with a glare of devilry as he looks up and says, "Angie Smith?"

My lips tilt up slightly. "Pleasure to meet you."

"Funny, sometimes you can tell because their name just fits them. I would never guess you for an Angie."

"Why would you say that?"

He taps his lower lip with a long, deft finger, and I'm instantly distracted by the thought of what that finger could do.

"I don't know. Just something told me that wasn't you. You and Ashley were the only two people I couldn't find any pictures of or any info on really. You guys are smart, or should I add, private."

"Let's go with private." I wink, which makes him raise his eyebrows. I can tell I'm the oldest in the class, and the mad professor here seems to be closer to my age, but I'm still trying to figure out what his name is. "Can I play your little game?"

His lips push together as he nods his head in interest. "By all means. Do you want the class list?"

"No, I bet I can guess your name."

His head moves up and down slowly. "Take your best shot." His arms open wide, allowing me to fully take in every part of him.

"Let's see. I know it starts with a C by my registration, but you have that whole nerdy, indie vibe going on, so I'm going to rule out Chris, Charlie, and Cameron." The barely noticeable lift to his lips tells me that neither of those is his name, so I start naming off every C name I can think of, waiting for any type of reaction to show in his features. "Christian, Caleb, Connor, Cody, Colin, Cole—" The twitch in his eye makes me stop. I pause, looking him up and down before slightly tilting my head in recognition. "Nice to meet you, Cole."

The grin covering his face makes me sit back in my chair. Yup, I'm made for this.

"Nicely done, Angie. The master gets beat at his own game. After class you're going to have to tell me more about how you did that."

"Anytime, *Professor Spence*," I say in a flirtatious way.

His eyes meet mine for what I think is a second too long for a student/ teacher moment, but I don't mind. When they break away, he addresses everyone else, "This course is going to be interactive, and I encourage participation. So, everyone get up, move closer, and gather around Mrs. Smith here." He returns my earlier wink before turning back around and writing his name across the board.

I'm intrigued by his lecture the entire night, and yeah, a lot of it was because he's easy on the eye. I also happen to love the way he challenges people and really gets us involved.

When he says good night, I turn to gather my things and am startled when I hear, "Angie, can I talk to you for a minute?"

My eyes meet with a fellow female student, who I shoot a smile before turning around. "Sure, Professor Spence."

As I approach his desk, he's gathering his paperwork to put into his backpack. He stops and turns to face me, leaning against the back of the desk and crossing his arms in front of his body. "So tell me, how did you guess my name?"

I tilt my head to the side, showing him the slightest grin. "Well, that's my little secret. Just like you said, though, you can learn a lot about a person if you pay close enough attention."

"I'm impressed. Still can't believe I got your name wrong. First time that little game didn't work out for me fully. Please tell me Angie isn't your real name. Give me some kind of hope."

I close my eyes, smiling but nodding my head slightly. "Okay, I'll give you that. Angie isn't my birth name. I legally changed it years ago." I can't believe I just told him that. No one here in San Francisco, or hell, in California, knows that Angie isn't my real name. For some reason, I felt comfortable enough in this moment to admit it.

"Okay, I feel a little bit better now, like I'm not a complete failure at my own game. But how did you know mine?"

"I was already trying to guess what it was before you even spoke. I guess I like to play little games, too."

He laughs. "That doesn't answer my question, though."

"I looked at what you were wearing, how you walked, your body type, the fact that you carry a Vans backpack instead of a briefcase." I pick up his backpack to prove my point. "Then, just like you, I paid attention and took a gamble. I guess you can say I'm good at reading facial expressions. You gave it away when your eye twitched slightly after I said Cole."

"Nicely done. You just might be cut out for this lawyer thing after all. So do I get to know your real name?"

I shake my head. "Nope, sorry. To you and everyone else, I'm Angie." I start to walk away but look over my shoulder. "No offense, though."

I hear him chuckle as he says, "None taken. See you Wednesday, Mrs. Smith."

I turn back again, giving him a quick smile before saying, "It's miss."

Chapter 2

CARTER

"You did not beat level thirteen on Super Mario Brothers," I say, throwing my arms up in mock disbelief, challenging Kyle, the eleven-year-old boy standing in front of me in the hospital rec room.

"I did! Look." He demands my attention toward the screen mounted high on the wall inside the playroom within the hospital.

"But you said that was impossible just a few days ago." I grab the beanbag from against the wall and sit next to him. "Show me." I nudge him with my shoulder.

I watch as he takes a serious game-playing stance, eyes glued to the screen, moving the controller up with every jump his character makes.

Seeing the enjoyment on his face lights up that dark spot in my heart. Working at UCSF Medical Center has changed me, both for the better and the worse. Seeing the fight in this kid's eyes keeps me going every day. Even when he knows his life is limited, he keeps a good attitude and plays, knowing that today might be the last if he doesn't find a donor soon.

After I sit with him for a few minutes, I nudge him again. "Hey, any chance I can get you to your room for a quick exam?"

He lets out a deep sigh. "Do we have to?"

"It's either with me while I'm on duty or who you refer to as Nurse Ratchet," I reply, tilting my head in question.

"I'll make you a deal," he says, acting all official. "You race me in Need for Speed, and if you win, you can examine me."

I squint my eyes in his direction, trying to appear intimidating as I say in a villainous voice, "You're on."

He hands me a remote, and we get down to our game. The cars fly around the track as the police try to catch us. He knocks me off the track, but I steal the wrench he needs to fix his car.

We're on the last loop, and I purposely throw the game by missing my turn and running hard into the wall.

As he crosses the finish line, he jumps up, throws the controller on the ground, and screams, "Woohoo," as he runs around the room. "I just beat Dr. Donovan!"

He's high fiving the other kids and parents as he runs the length of the room, and I stand up, knowing this is probably too much, and he's going to crash soon.

I was right.

His face goes pale, and I race over to him.

"Hey, bud, enough celebration for today." I pause to look into his eyes, making sure he's okay before continuing, "Didn't your parents ever teach you it's not nice to gloat?" I tease, trying to ease the situation and not make a huge deal so he can enjoy his moment.

I walk him to a wheelchair and guide him into the seat as he says, "You lost fair and square. Now write it." He points to the board at our running tally of games and winners.

I don't throw every game, just ones I can tell need to happen. This poor kid is not doing well, and I want him to have better days in any small way I can help. Medically, this is our last hope, so yeah, I let him win a game here and there.

"Come on, can I walk you back to your room?" I ask, leaning down so I'm eye to eye with him.

"But I won! No exam needed," he fights back.

"Yeah, well, next time, don't run around the room, and I won't force the subject. You and I both know you might have passed out there in the end, and now I'm forced to play the doctor role."

"Damn doctor," he deadpans.

I eye him, questioning his use of language.

"Damn is not a bad word. I hear my dad say it all the time," he states matter-of-factly.

I laugh while starting to roll his chair, disregarding his statement and guiding him back to his room to check his vitals.

These kids have become my life. I never planned on being a pediatric oncologist, but when the residency at UCSF came up, something called to me, so I applied. When I got in, I knew this was where I needed to be.

Becoming a doctor was a dream of mine for years, and when I got a scholarship to UCLA, I knew all my dreams were going to come true. It was the opportunity of a lifetime to get out of our middle-of-nowhere town and make something of myself.

Living in San Francisco is so different than the small Minnesota town I grew up in. It took a little getting used to, but I've grown to love it here. Well, I guess I should say I've grown to love the hospital. Outside of here, I don't have much of a life, just my one friend, and my one hobby. That's enough for me.

As I listen to Kyle's heartbeat, I look up into his eyes. They're slightly glazed over. He's tired, too tired for a kid who should be running around in the park, playing soccer, and developing his first crush.

A nurse comes in with his daily meds, so I rough his hair around and say goodbye. We exchange our secret handshake; one we developed together a few weeks ago when he wouldn't even let me examine him.

Sometimes, the sickest ones become the weariest. It took a little while to earn his trust, let him know I wasn't here to just stick a needle in his arm and turn him into a lab rat.

I care. Maybe I care too much. Who knows.

I write down my notes regarding Kyle's collapse to his checkup and leave it at the nurse's station. Looking at the large clock on the wall, I see my shift is over. I should get some sleep, but I opt to do one more round and say goodnight to the kids.

My life is great except for the one thing missing. I glance at the inside of my wrist and the reminder of what was once mine.

Chapter 3

EVANGELINE

Sleep is something that eludes me. I blame it on the curse of being female. I wish I could shut my brain off like a switch but not tonight. One thought leads to the next, and before I know it, I'm wracking my brain, wondering how I got to my current thought only to end up backtracking to how I ended up where I did.

All when I should be sleeping.

Tonight is one of the worst nights because somehow I ended up thinking about him—Carter.

He keeps sneaking into my thoughts ever since the other day when Kaitlyn tagged me in that photo. It's been ten years since I left my life and started over. I've been tempted so many times to search for him, but I've always fought the urge. Now that I know he's out there, I feel like everything's changed.

I haven't even turned on Facebook for that reason. I'm terrified to go down that road, relive those memories, reveal those truths.

"Let's get out of here." I feel his breath against my skin as he whispers into my ear. His hands run down my arms, and he folds them around mine.

I look around the field of open tailgates and all of our friends hanging out, partying under the shine of the moonlight. Kaitlyn gives me a knowing smile before grabbing our friends, Tammy and Liz, to leave us alone.

Carter and I have been together for about a month, and even though he's leaving for college in a few months, we've been getting closer and closer every day. We just get each other. I'm the crazy one who's breaking him out of his shell, and he's the calm one who keeps me in line; well, sometimes. We're quickly learning that we complete one another and bring out the best traits in the other person.

While I may be the outgoing girl, who does and says whatever she likes when the crowd is around, with him I'm…different. I don't feel like I have to be on at all times. Sometimes it's nice to sit back and just exist.

We can hang out, just talking for hours. I listen to his stories, and by the end of the night, I'm curled up in his arms, right where I belong.

I like it. I like him.

Turning to give him my full attention, I ask, "What do you have in mind?"

"Me, you, on a blanket under the stars down by the lake."

"Do you now?" I wrap my arms around his neck. "And you think I'm gonna follow you down there, just because you asked?"

"Will it help if I say please?" He raises his eyebrows as his lips show a hint of a smirk.

My head falls back in a laugh. "You're too cute. You know that, right?"

"Yeah, I do. So, what do you say?" He looks me right in my eyes as he lifts his hand to tuck a stray hair behind my ear. "I don't want to if you don't want to."

"What if I say I want to?"

"Then I say let's get out of here." He leans down and meets his lips with mine as he picks me up and slowly walks me back to his truck.

This is it. We're bringing this relationship to the next level, and when I look back at him, I have no doubt that I'm ready for this. For him. For us.

Fuck me! I rise out of bed and tug on the roots of my hair.

I can't. I can't do this to myself.

Not again.

Before I change my mind, I pick up my phone, click on the Facebook app, and delete my account. That part of me is dead. Who I was back then is long gone, and I can never go back.

I walk into the bathroom and splash cold water on my face, waking myself up from the dreams that plague me even when I'm wide awake.

Running my hands down my cheeks, I assess myself in the mirror. The blue eyes staring back at me are from that same girl who fell in love with a boy in the back of a pick-up truck. But the soul behind them is older, wiser… scarred.

I let out a long surge of air from deep within my lungs. I vowed never to lose another moment dwelling on the pain.

With a smile, I look at the new Angie reflecting back at me. The me of today.

"No more dwelling," I tell myself. "And no more memories."

"Kamii girl, what you got for me today?" I ask as I walk into her office without knocking. We gave up formalities a while ago, and I love how easygoing she has become. Today doesn't look like her day, though, and when she looks up tears spill from her eyes. "Why the tears?" I walk faster to her desk and try to comfort her.

"Stupid hormones." She laughs. "I was looking at the calendar, realizing I'm only a few weeks out, and I don't have anything ready."

I'm still shocked to see the huge belly pushing out from Kamii's little body. I can't help but smile every time I see her. Not even a year ago she was a workaholic, quiet, keep to herself, kick-ass attorney, and now, she's everything she never was—except the kick-ass attorney part. She amazes me at every turn.

She's getting ready for her next case, only this one doesn't need to be solved, and there's no owner's manual attached. I can tell she's a little freaked out about her baby girl arriving soon, but I know with Preston's help she'll do just fine.

"But what about the baby shower? You got a ton of stuff from everyone at the firm," I remind her.

"I have no clue what to do with all of it. It's all still sitting in the nursery. I'm a wreck."

I grab a tissue and hand it to her. "You'll be fine. Don't stress. What can I do to help?"

She looks up like a light bulb went off in her head with the best idea she's ever had, and now I'm scared. I don't know why I offered to help. I'm happy for Kamii, especially with her past, but I've tried my hardest not to get involved in anything related to her pregnancy.

"We don't have anything on the schedule today, do we?" she asks with a devilish grin.

Well, crap. "Um." I look down at the notebook I'm holding, praying something magically appeared without my knowing it. "Nope, we sure don't," I say with a little fear in my voice that I'm trying to hide.

"Yay! We can set up the nursery and have a total girly day."

Shit. First I see Carter on Facebook and now this? *Why is life torturing me this way?*

Kamii looks so hopeful. I know I can't say no, but I don't know if I can do this.

Looks like I don't have a choice, though. Not waiting for my reply, she gets up and grabs her purse. "Come on, this is just what I needed today. I guess they call it nesting. I don't understand all of this, but having you there will be fun."

I grin, doing my best to fake my excitement as we walk out of her office, grab my stuff, and head to her house. This might just push me over the edge.

CARTER

I hate this Throwback Thursday hashtag. If I wanted to relive those days, I would. I don't need Facebook reminding me of it weekly. That was another time, another world that I've fought hard to find again but have never found.

Funny enough, Cole, someone I met years ago when I was trying to find my past, is the only real friend I have now. He was volunteering at the student law center when I went in to research my options. After helping me a few times, we ran into each other at a bar and started to hang out from there.

About a year ago, he brought me into a club—a secret club—that is helping me finally move on from my past.

He's way more outgoing than I am, and we tend to stick together when we're there. Not that we're into each other in that way, it's just more fun to watch one girl with two guys. The way their bodies react and they lose their minds gets me off more than I'll ever be able to explain.

And it's enough for me.

That's why Club Bridge has been exactly what I needed in my life; the one thing that provides the perfect distraction.

But this picture on Facebook that I can't seem to get out of my mind is taking everything away from me.

I saw it the other morning, commented, but then shut it as quickly as I could, not wanting to feel the ache I always get when I see her there. There were twelve people in the photo, and of course, only ten were tagged. I've looked everywhere for her, but it looks like Kaitlyn hasn't found her either. I didn't bother looking at who else was tagged, just saw that the number was lower than eleven, so I didn't bother.

Against my better judgment, I put on *Falling Inside the Black* by Skillet. The song has been my go-to when I'm in a funk caused by her. Where women put on sad, sappy songs to listen to, I put on this. It describes my situation so much and makes me feel like I'm not crazy still holding onto all this pain and resentment. Tonight, though, I feel like a complete glutton for punishment, and I do one better than the song—I pull up the photo again. This time, though, I notice there are only nine people tagged now, instead of ten.

The thought makes my insides clench from the unknown. I couldn't imagine that she'd been tagged and somehow, I didn't know. It was torture to think I had her that close and hadn't paid attention.

I start my search all over again. Checking for her name first and then going through every single one of Kaitlyn's friends. After an hour, the strain in my neck hurts just as bad as the pain in my heart. I wonder if I'll ever find her.

Staring at the photo, I wonder how much she's changed. If it's anything like I have, I wonder if I'd even recognize her. I've changed a lot since that photo was taken. I was still a scrawny, twig of a boy, shocked that my crush for all those years was finally giving me the time of day.

After high school, I grew a few more inches and spent a lot of time at the gym to get my frustrations out. I can easily say I'm twice the size I was then. The mop on my head was longer compared to the buzz cut I sport now, and of course, I didn't have any of the tattoos then. The one thing that hasn't changed, though, is the tattoo on the inside of my wrist. No matter how much shit Cole has given me over the years for it, I'd never change anything about it. It's the only tie I have left to her.

The sight of it catches my attention, and instantly, I close my eyes, taking a deep breath when I'm brought back to that night. It was so perfect. We were perfect. She said we'd be together again, and this tattoo would represent the starting line one day. She winked at me when she said that, and I wonder if she already knew. The thought pisses me off. I stand up, running my fingers through my hair and down my face before grabbing my keys to head out for the night. Thankfully, it's Thursday, and the club is open.

I only attend on Thursday and Saturday nights. Friday the club has more of a BDSM atmosphere, and that's not my thing, so I stay away.

I send a quick text to Cole to make sure he's on his way as well. I don't have to have him there. I'm just in the mood to blow some steam, and he's the one who puts all the effort into lining someone up for us. I get to stand back and not talk much but get to participate in the fun.

The women like the mystery of it all, so I run with it. Whatever gets them off, gets me off, so I'm not one to complain.

Chapter 4

Evangeline

"Angie?" I hear Kamii yell from her office.

I was just about to pack up my things for the night, but instead, I click off my screen and walk toward her office.

Standing in her doorway, I watch as she attempts to pick something up. Finally giving up, she asks, "Can you please pick up the pen I dropped over here?"

The laugh I'm trying to hide sneaks through as I walk up to her, grab the pen, and put it on her desk. "Was that all you needed?"

She shoots me a glare, clearly stating not to mock her. Yet, we both fall into a fit of giggles in a matter of seconds. "I'm such a mess. When will this baby just come out already? She *needs* to come out."

I offer her a reassuring smile. "Just a little while longer. She's not done cooking, yet."

"I'm so over this, but here, sit. I wanted to see if you have plans tonight."

"Not really. What are we working on?"

She takes a deep breath, pulling her fingers up to her lip where she starts to lightly tug. I've been working with her for years, and this is her tell-tale sign; something's wrong.

"What's going on here? What's up with the lip thing?" I ask.

Her fingers drop instantly. "What? Nothing?"

"Kamii, you only tug on your lip when it's something serious. What's wrong?"

"Ugh! Preston says the same thing. Am I that obvious? I'm an attorney. I run courtrooms, yet with my personal life, it seems people can read me like a book."

I grin because what she's saying is so true, but that's beside the fact. "So really, what's up?"

"Preston and I need your help, and we were hoping you could have drinks with us tonight?"

"Sure, whatever you guys need. Where should I meet you?"

"Here, help me up and let's walk to Rickhouse. Lord knows I need to walk as much as I can."

When we arrive, Preston is already seated in a booth in the back, and we head toward his table. I love the way his face brightens when he sees us walking up.

The love they share is evident more and more every time I see them. I know there's more to their story than what Kamii's told me, but I've tried not to pry too much.

After he says hello to his wife and leans down to talk to his unborn daughter, he turns to me. "What can I get you to drink, Angie?"

"I'll take a Dirty Shirley, please," I respond as I slide into the booth, and Preston walks to the bar.

"Shut up. You're kidding me, right?" Kamii almost yells in disbelief.

I point my finger, daring her to challenge me. "What's wrong with that? Don't make fun like I haven't grown up because I still like my kiddie drink." It wouldn't be the first time someone made fun of my drink of choice, but I don't care. I loved Shirley Temples as a child, and now, I love them with vodka.

"No, it has nothing to do with that. It's just—" She takes a deep breath. "I knew you were perfect for what I'm about to ask you, and you just proved it right there."

"With my drink order?"

"Yes, with a simple drink order." She lets out a laugh as she wipes a small tear that slipped out of her right eye. "My close friend, Becca, used to order Dirty Chai at Starbucks, and I've always said you reminded me of her. Did I ever tell you exactly how Preston and I met?"

"No, actually, I've never heard. I assumed you knew him before the murder case last year, but I never wanted to get into your personal life too much."

She laughs almost nervously. "Yeah, it might shock you a bit, but that's why I want to talk to you."

She reaches up for her lip again, and when I give her a squinted look, she drops her hand, shaking her head. "Yes, you're perfect for this. So, Preston owns something no one knows he owns, not even the people there."

"Huh? His construction company?" I ask, confused.

"No, this one is really private…a members only type of thing."

"Okay, so do you want me to join or something?"

"Um, well." She looks around like she's nervous about something. "You see, we need help when the baby is born."

"I'm not sure what kind of help I can be. I mean, I don't know anything about running a business or anything."

"If there's one thing I've learned about you these past years, it's that I love how open you are…sexually."

Now it's my time to laugh. That's probably the understatement of the year, and I'm not afraid to show it. Kamii and I work so closely together, and I tend to overshare or have become the queen of TMI.

I have absolutely no desire to be in a relationship, and I love to have sex, so I have a little—okay, a lot of fun with whomever I choose at the time. Oh, and I love to talk about it.

I forget sometimes that people aren't like me, and I tend to make them feel uncomfortable about it. I've never gotten that vibe from Kamii, especially more recently, but I still have no clue where this is going.

"You know I love sex, and I love to talk about it, but what does this have to do with anything?"

"This business of his is called Bridge. It's an, um, a…" She closes her eyes, looking like she's afraid to say what's to come. When she opens them, looking straight into mine, she blurts out, "Fuck it, it's an anonymous sex club."

My jaw drops. "Are you serious right now?"

Kamii covers her eyes, and I can see her face turning red as a tomato under her hands.

"Is that how you met him?" I ask in disbelief.

She nods her head, not removing her hands. "Yes, that's how I knew he was innocent and being framed. We were together at the club the night the murder happened."

I reach out and remove her hands for her. "I'm so fucking in love with you right now."

She grins, and I can see the red slowly start to disappear from her face.

"Seriously, I'm seeing you in a whole new light," I say through a chuckle.

"Please don't look at me any differently."

"Oh no, not like that. I'm excited to hear you're really just like me. You like to be fucked, and you like it kinky. I'm beyond thrilled right now to call you my friend."

"Jeez, please, keep your voice down," she whispers as she looks around, and the crimson color creeps back up her face.

Just then Preston approaches our table with a smirk. "So, I take it you told her?"

"Hell yeah, she did. Preston, my man." I shake my head, looking back and forth between him and her. "You two just officially became my favorite couple."

"So, you'll do it?" he asks with hope lacing his tone.

"Wait, do I get to join?" I ask, coming out of my seat in excitement.

"Yes, we're hoping you'll join and keep an eye on things for us while we aren't there. You'll get a free membership. There's not much to do, but we just like having someone there who can pay attention while no one knows who they are."

I pick up my glass, holding it up to toast them both. "You don't have to ask me twice. Here's to the best job I'll ever have."

Chapter 5

EVANGELINE

"Front and center again, I see," Professor Spence states with a quick smile covering his face before he wipes it away.

"What can I say, I like to be the center of attention," I respond as I sit up straighter in my chair and fluff my hair, over exaggerating my comment.

"I can tell you are quite often," he whispers as he walks by, giving me a quick glance before heading toward another student.

Did my teacher really just flirt with me? Well then, this class just took a turn in a direction I can't wait to explore. He's sexy even though I've never gone for the retro, glasses type, but he's definitely worth looking into more. I wonder if there's some policy against us dating, though.

He turns around and catches me checking him out, but I don't turn my head or pretend I wasn't. I've never been shy about who I am or who I like. If he's going to flirt, I'll give it right back. Shit, he'd know the rules better than I would. It's not my job on the line.

"Tonight, we're going to talk about stereotypes, judging a book by its cover, per se. In the judicial system, everyone is innocent until proven guilty, or so they say. But what happens when someone is judged to be guilty just by the way they look? Take Angie here." He looks at me with his hand held out, and his pointer finger curled up like he's summoning me toward him. "Come to the front for a quick second."

I squint my eyes, getting the feeling he's up to no good but follow his lead and approach him, eyeing him suspiciously before I turn to face the rest of the class.

"Alex, point out something that's obvious about Angie."

"She's sexy as hell," he blurts out, and I instantly blow him a kiss in return as my thank you.

"Why, yes." Professor Spence looks down at my tight gray pants and over the knee boots that make my legs look ten times longer than they really are. "But give me more. Just by the way she looks, without knowing anything else about her, would you say she's single or married?"

"Definitely single, and on the prowl," Alex teases.

"So a girl in a relationship can't dress nicely?" he responds.

"Not girls that I know," Alex states matter-of-factly, which gets a soft chuckle from the rest of the class.

"Okay, how about you, Nichole? Tell me, do you think she grew up in the City, in California, or somewhere else?"

Nichole pauses, looking me up and down for any clues. "I'm going to say somewhere outside of California."

"Interesting. Why do you say that?"

"Well, she's older than I am—sorry, just stating a fact," she says directly to me before continuing, which I just shrug off. "But still young enough to be fashionable and obviously not on a shoe-string, college budget. I get the feeling she lives here now, which has introduced her to more of the fashion world than wherever she grew up. That's why she still wants to look this way like she hasn't been able to dress like this her entire life."

He nods in confirmation. "Very good, way to think deeper than what's in plain sight. So how old do you think she is?"

"I'm going to guess late twenties," she says, unsure of herself like she's trying not to offend me.

A small laugh escapes my lips before I regain my composure.

"Okay, one more. Sonia, give me something else you see just by looking at her."

"Um…" She thinks for a second, so I turn around, holding out my arms, putting myself on display even more. "Because she's a little older than us, taking a night class and obviously dressed nicer than every single person here, I'm guessing she already has a full-time job where she works in an office setting and has to dress more professionally."

"Oh, good point. Okay, Angie, how did everyone do?" Professor Spence asks.

"Well, I am single, I grew up in a small town far from here, I'm twenty-eight, and yes, I work at a law firm during the day, so that's why I'm enrolled in night classes."

"Well then, I say the class did pretty well reading your so-called book," he says to me before addressing the class again. "So you see, there are more ways to get information out of people than looking them up on social media. We were trying to guess these things about Angie here, and she willingly gave us more answers than we planned. She could have just said you were right or wrong, but she gave us actual specifics without us having to ask. Sometimes you can extract the info out of people without trying." He leans in to whisper in my ear, "I knew I'd find out more about you somehow." Then he walks to the board to write something as I return to my seat, trying to hide the feeling running through my veins.

Yes, he's definitely flirting with me, and I'm so game.

After class, I approach his desk once the room clears out, and only a few students linger in the back. "Nice little trick you pulled there." His face says it all, so I keep talking, "Do I get to play your game, again?"

He zips up his bag before leaning against his desk in a sexy-as-hell, laid-back way. "What do you want to know?"

"How about we level the playing field, and I get to know everything about you that you know about me, and nothing more."

"Sounds like a fun game. I'm in." He pauses like he's waiting for me to say something.

"So…spill it."

"I'm thirty-one. Single. I grew up not far from here, and I'm an associate attorney at a law firm, trying to work my way up."

"So why do you teach then?" I ask.

"Why are you taking this class then? It's an answer for an answer, right?"

I grin, seeing how fun this game is going to be. "We'll see how far this goes." I start to walk away. "Night, Professor Spence."

"It's Cole, by the way."

"I know, but I like Professor Spence better." I wink before completely turning around to leave.

Chapter 6

EVANGELINE

Tonight is the night I finally get my first look at Club Bridge, and Kamii is treating me to dinner first to go over the last of the details. I didn't get to actually visit it yet, but all of my paperwork has been filled out, and I took the necessary tests last week. They said I could go and watch, but that sounded like pure torture—not being able to actually join in on the fun.

"So how does this work again? I honestly get to fuck whoever I want tonight?" I ask after we eat, getting right to the point and putting it out there.

Kamii shakes her head almost in disbelief. "God, you're too much like my friend Becca…the girl who brought me into the club. So yes and no. You don't have to, and I encourage you to look around, take everything in, and get a feel for the place. I didn't, um…" She leans in whispering, "have sex with anyone my first time."

"Are you really shy about this? *Um, have sex*," I jokingly mock her. "Really, Kamii? This, at a club, is plain, old, simple fucking, all day long."

She shakes her head, covering her eyes. "Yes. I guess it is, but you'll see. Some people will already be paired up, and some will be eyeing you. You're fresh meat, so let that sink in. Try to be choosy your first time. It's more overwhelming than you think. Do you have a name picked out for yourself?"

"Yes. Evangeline."

She looks at me suspiciously, like she knows it means something. "Care to explain why?"

"No. Not really." I shrug.

"Most people use names that are totally different than their own; mine is Eurydice, from Greek mythology. Are you sure you want to use something that could be a real name?"

"Let's just say it reminds me of something I want to be, and this club might just be the answer to getting me there."

"Okay then, Evangeline it is. Do you have your mask?"

I pull out a magenta mask that covers my forehead all the way to my nose in a solid black material with a lace overlay and a lace butterfly that sticks off the mask. It's cute, sexy, and I felt it covered my face the most. If I'm going to do this, I don't want to have to worry about the guy recognizing me at Starbucks the next day.

"Wow, that's beautiful," Kamii says as she reaches out to touch the butterfly.

"Thanks, I thought so, and it's my favorite color, so it was perfect."

"It's totally you. Just one word of advice…There's always a human factor you have to deal with. Feelings, jealousy, no matter how anonymous we keep it, things can happen, so my best advice to you is to keep the club at the club."

I nod, knowing I'll have no problem distinguishing between the two. I don't do relationships, which is why this whole anonymous thing is perfect for me.

"Well then, what do you say? Are you ready?" she asks.

"Hell, yes, I'm ready. Let's do this."

The guards at the front door know who I am, but no names are exchanged or introductions made. Just seeing I'm with Kamii says everything they need to know, and my entrance is granted.

I take off my maroon dress to reveal my black lace bustier with magenta accents to match my mask. It sits right above my waist, and the garter belt straps hang past my lace thong and attach to a pair of simple, sheer black stockings.

I look over at Kamii to see her wearing the cutest baby doll nighty, showing off her belly in the most tasteful way. Preston must have been watching the door. Before I know it, a tall man has his arm wrapped around her from the back, embracing her belly and kissing her neck in a move so seductive I turn my head, not wanting to feel like I'm intruding on their time together.

Then I remember why I'm here and that I'll see a lot of that tonight, but knowing it's Preston and Kamii somehow makes it different. With that thought, I make sure my mask is on correctly, take a deep breath, and enter what I hope to be a new world for me to indulge in.

I've dreamed of what this place would be like since they first told me, but nothing prepared me for this. Kamii wanted to go a little later, so I wouldn't be one of the first to arrive, and now everything makes total sense.

Everywhere I look, I see something I never thought I'd ever experience. I envisioned what it would be like to physically watch people having sex, but nothing compares to actually seeing it live, right in front of me. I can't help but stare, opening my mouth slightly as my skin starts to flush with nervousness and excitement I can't begin to explain other than it's like nothing I've felt before.

Most of the scenes have already begun, and very few people line the areas in between. I secretly praise Kamii for making me wait till later to arrive. This way I get to see exactly how this all goes down without the whole wondering how and when.

As I stand in a big open room, I see five areas surrounding me, all with people engaging in some kind of sexual act on different things from beds to couches to tables that look like they're padded in some way. In front of those areas sit a few random people who are obviously here just to watch.

I keep trying to look at each scene, but it's a crazy weird feeling to watch people I don't know have sex. So instead, I look at the people sitting by themselves. To my surprise, the expression on their faces turns me on more than the people actually having sex, so for now, I turn all my attention toward them.

It's the way their faces tighten around their eyes, and their lips push together just slightly that pinches my chest in anticipation. But what gets me the most is the way their bodies move just slightly enough to where someone not paying attention wouldn't even notice, like they themselves aren't aware they're doing it. But Lord-almighty, it sends tingles down my body, pooling in my favorite spot.

I think Kamii was right. I'm a little overwhelmed by this all, and the thought of sitting back only to watch tonight sounds good for the first time today.

I'm allowed two drinks, so I order my Dirty Shirley and look around for which scene I want to take in first.

Each one has something different going on; some with only two people, some with five or even six people. One catches my eye, and I walk toward the open side room with two men and one woman. I've never had a threesome, but the idea sounds perfect to break me in per se.

As I sit down, I take in the girl wrapped in both men. All three of them are completely naked and well into the scene. The thing that stands out the most is the way both men are absolutely enthralled by the one female. They don't look like they're there just to get off. No. The way their hands caress her body, the way they hold on to her, providing her security while they take her to another level makes a slow burn blaze low in my belly.

My mind starts to drift as I envision myself with these two men. I imagine what their hands would feel like on my body at the same time. Or what it would feel like to be fucked while my hands and mouth were busy on another guy's dick.

The thought excites me, enables me, and helps me make up my mind. I'll wait for my first time until I can be with two men. But not any two men. These two men.

Until then, I'll sit here, get my fill, and possibly enter another area to take care of myself.

Chapter 7

CARTER

Whack! The ball smacks hard against the bat, flying into the net before I reposition and get ready for the next ball. I swing hard, missing, and then throw my bat down in frustration. "Fuck!"

"Dude, calm down. What's up with you today?" Cole asks from outside the cage.

I shake my head. "Just need to blow off some steam."

"Yeah, that was obvious. What happened today? 'Cause I know you blew a lot of steam last night." He laughs.

"Just frustrated about work."

"What? Is saving kids getting to you now?" he taunts.

I sigh and drop my head. That's what I should be doing. But with Kyle I can't and it's tearing me apart. Gaining my composure, I'm ready for the next ball. "If only it were that easy," I bark out as I hit it hard.

"Need to talk about it?"

"There's not much to talk about." I stop batting and walk out of the cage before continuing. "There's this kid who's really sick, and there's not a damn thing I can do about it."

"Why not? I thought you were all superhero status," he mocks me.

"Not on this one. He needs a bone-marrow donor, and we haven't found a match."

"Then you haven't looked hard enough," he states like it's that easy.

"We've been searching, but no luck so far."

"Have you held one of those donor drive things?"

"No, I haven't, but companies do them all the time."

"If you haven't found a match, maybe you should put your energy toward putting one together yourself instead of taking it out on the poor ball over there."

I drop my head, my shoulders moving up and down with my inner chuckle. Cole's always one to make me smile when I feel there's nothing to smile about.

"You might be on to something."

"Of course I am. I'm me."

"Okay, that's enough of your ego today."

"Nope, not even close. Watch this," he boasts as he enters the cage. He gets ready to swing the bat and then hits it hard into the net.

When I mentioned the donor drive to our supplier, they were more than happy to help out. We picked a day for a few weeks away, and now, I need to get the word out, so I call Cole again. After the batting cages, we put together a plan, and he called his law firm to see if they'd be interested in getting involved as well.

"Okay, we're all set. Can you help me with a flier, so all your information is on there correctly with the firm?" I say into the phone after he answers.

"I'm on it. Email me the info and a picture of him so I can put it on there. We've already set it up with our web guy, and he's going to blast it to everyone we know, and then I can print the flier to post it all over the campus."

"Right on. Hey, Cole." I pause. "Thanks for helping out. It means a lot."

"You know I'm here. I got you," he says before hanging up.

I head to Kyle's room to tell him the good news and get a picture. When I walk in his parents are there. "Mr. and Mrs. Bradshaw, how's our little patient?" I ask, holding out my hand to greet them.

"I'm not little!" Kyle bites back, making us all laugh.

"Sorry, of course you're not." I hold my arms up in surrender.

"He's hanging in there. Been complaining of a stomach ache," his dad speaks up.

"Yeah, that's a side effect of the meds we have him on. I'll see if we can get him something for that. I came in here with some good news, though." His parents turn their attention fully to me. These days, any good news is more than welcome, and it shows on their faces.

"My buddy and I are putting on a donor drive to search for a match. He even got his law firm to sponsor the event."

"That's amazing." His mom walks over to hug me.

"Let's just hope we find someone." I hug her back then turn to Kyle. "Till then, I think we're due for a rematch. Let me finish my rounds, and I'll come back for you."

"You got it. I'll be here," Kyle says with excitement in his eyes.

"Oh, I almost forgot. Can I get a picture of you to put on the flier we're making to hand out for the drive?"

"Ugh, really? Do I have to?"

"Now, Kyle, this is a really cool thing they're doing for you. Be nice," his mom says to him.

"Fine. But only if you're in it too," Kyle says to me.

I shrug. "That's all I have to do? Man, I'm going to try to keep this tactic in mind for the future."

He gives me a don't-try look. He's not always the easiest patient but, for being a young kid, his courage is amazing.

His mom holds up my camera, and I squeeze in next to him on the bed, wrapping my arm around his little body. We smile big for the picture I hope will pull on people's heartstrings and prompt them to come get tested.

Chapter 8

EVANGELINE

"So...?" Kamii taunts as she greets me when I enter her office. "What did you think about last night? I didn't see you hook up with anyone before we left. Did you take my advice?"

I sit down, smiling at her. "I thought you were crazy when you said to watch the first time I was there, but when I walked in, I guess I was more surprised with it all than I thought I'd be."

"Oh yeah, I remember my first night." Her eyes glaze over with memories of her past. "Did you see anyone you were interested in at least?"

"Yes, two guys, actually."

"Two guys? Wait, were they together, with just one girl?"

"Yeah, you know who I'm talking about?"

She smiles brightly like she has a hidden secret but keeps it to herself, instead saying, "Well then, look at you." She leans back in her chair. "So are you going back tonight?"

"No, I may like kinky things, but the whole BDSM world isn't for me."

"They won't be there anyway, so you're in luck. They only come on Thursday and Saturday nights."

"Are they always together?"

"Yup. Not with each other that way, but always them and one girl."

I eye her smirk before starting in. "You fucked them!"

She goes to cover her guilty-as-sin face but reaches down instead, grabbing her stomach. "Holy schmoly!" she states in shock as she grits her teeth together tightly.

I quickly stand up and walk around her desk where she's hunched over. "What's wrong?"

She takes a few seconds to recover before inhaling a deep breath and then sits back in her chair. "I've been having sharp pains off and on all morning. I thought they were just Braxton Hicks but that one was different."

"Just relax and I'll go get you some water."

I leave the room and walk to the water cooler, pouring her a cup. Before I make it back to her office, I hear her yelp in pain again, so I run to see her standing, gripping the table so hard it looks like she's going to break it off.

"You have to breathe, Kamii. Don't hold it in. You'll make it worse."

She shakes her head defiantly, not saying a word until the contraction has passed, and she turns her head to look at me with fear written all over her face.

I take a deep breath, trying to calm her down with my motions. "Hun, I think you're in labor," I say, walking over to her desk and placing the water down.

"I'm scared," she whispers, squinting her eyes.

I rub her back. "I know. You got this, girl. Let's call Preston and get you to a hospital."

"Please come with me," she begs, gripping my arm.

Shit. This is the last thing I want to be involved in. I don't know if I can take it. When my eyes meet hers, though, I know I can't say no, so I don't. Instead, I nod. Holding my breath as I stand her up, I pray to God I'm strong enough to do this.

When we got to the hospital, Kamii begged for me to be in the room with her.

The monitor next to the bed shows a spiked line, meaning Kamii's contractions are hitting hard. Sweat pours down the side of her face. She's squeezing her eyes and gritting her teeth as the spike continues to climb.

I want to tell her the pain will fade soon, that once the baby is out it will all pass, and she'll hardly remember the feeling, but I don't.

Instead, I rub her head and help her count, encouraging her to breathe until the line begins to fall, and she's offered a brief reprieve until the next.

The contractions are coming fast, and relief floods through me when Preston walks through the door. I try to back out of the room, but the contractions are coming fast, and the nurse stops me, saying, "Grab a leg, honey. She's ready to push."

I'm stuck here, struggling with the choice of being a good friend or protecting my own heart.

Closing my eyes, I force all my pain down. That deep ache I feel pinching low in my chest on a daily basis tries to explode like a volcano. I knew it would someday.

I've kept it there for so long, and I try even harder to channel all that pain into as much support as I can give to my friend.

It only takes fifteen minutes, and Kamii's beautiful baby girl is born, making my tears fall even faster. When they place the little angel on her body, my knees weaken, and I have to grip the bed before I fall over.

The tiny baby's skin is red, and she has a big, beautiful cry. The sound is like a siren to my dreams and a memory I'll never forget. I can't hold the pain back anymore.

The look on Kamii's face as she glances down at her miracle and then up at Preston just about does me in.

The sight of the tattoo on my wrist makes my heart ache even more. Normally I have it covered by either a bracelet or a watch, but it got in the way of holding her leg, so I removed it and put it in my pocket.

This is all too much.

I kiss Kamii on the head, congratulate Preston, and leave the room before I'm pushed over an edge I can't come back from.

When my phone rings the next day showing Kamii calling, guilt runs through my chest and bubbles in my stomach. I know I shouldn't have left when I did, but I had to. I just hope one day she understands.

Now my hand hovers over the decline button for the second time today, but my heart can't do it, so I take a deep breath and bring my phone up to my ear. "How's my newest mommy friend doing?" I ask as my voice is a dead giveaway.

She recognizes it, and I hear her sigh into the phone. "Spill it, girl. Why'd you bail yesterday?"

I close my eyes, fighting the burn I know is coming behind my lids, thankful she can't see me.

"Kamii, come on. Tell me about little Becca."

I can almost hear her smile, but she doesn't let me off that easily. "Don't dodge the subject, but she's amazing. So tiny. So perfect."

"Is she nursing?"

"Yes, but answer my question."

I pause, biting my lower lip to stop the trembling that I'm sure will form soon. "Kamii, can we just pretend I didn't and move on?"

She sighs. "Fine, as long as you get your butt down here."

I inhale a deep breath, filling my lungs, waiting for the sting I thought would come at the thought, but it never does.

Maybe I can finally do this, and everything is just in my head.

"Okay, you got a deal. I'll be there shortly."

We hang up, and I lay on my bed, twirling my hair in my fingers as my head plays tricks on my heart. I've been able to avoid anything like this for years, but that wasn't by coincidence.

I have friends here in San Francisco, but I've been careful not to take those friendships to the next level. All of them are single, and we like to go dancing, drinking, and pick up new guys.

Whenever a friend got serious with a guy or even got pregnant, I'd slowly fade away from their life and meet new friends at a bar or club. I don't do it to be a bitch; I do it to protect my heart.

Yes, it can be lonely sometimes, but it's also uncomplicated. And hey, it keeps my world drama free. It can be nice—I always have something new to look forward to.

The longer I lie here, the more I can feel my heart growing and actually being okay with this, even slightly excited to see my friend's new baby.

When I arrive at the hospital, I look around, stalling briefly to make sure the fear I was scared of overtaking me doesn't come on by surprise. Relief fills me when none forms.

I honestly think I can do this.

With a renewed purpose, I take a deep breath as I walk down the hall and into Kamii's room. The vision of her sitting with her baby, wrapped in her arms as she plays with her little finger fills me with hope, not fear.

Tears slipping from my eyes are a welcome feeling of happiness as I walk over to see my friend's newest miracle.

Chapter 9

CARTER

For the third time, I hear pounding on my door, but just like the other two times, I ignore it. Instead, I turn the music up louder from my remote as I take my couch pillow and cover my face while lying down on my back.

The song I have on repeat plays again, and I hear someone storm into my apartment, turning off *Falling Inside the Black*.

"Man, not this shit again. How long have I known you?" Cole spits out.

"Turn it back on," I grunt, removing the pillow only to glare at him, daring him to say anything else about her before placing it back over my face.

He stares at me, shaking his head in frustration. "Bro, I'm just looking out for you. It's time to move on."

Move on. Fuck, if only he knew what I had, then maybe he'd get it.

"Come on, let's do it. Just me and you. No one's around." Evangeline grabs *my arms, trying to convince me to strip naked.*

"That lake is freezing," I fight back.

"Oh, come on. It's not that cold."

"Says the girl with no balls. They'll freeze off."

"Stop. No, they won't." She pushes back and slowly starts to pull her shirt up over her head. When it's completely off, she steps farther away, throwing it in my

direction before she slowly pulls down the jeans she's wearing.

A few hours ago we walked across the stage, graduating from our small high school. We were on our way to Grad Night at the school campus, but she pulled off at the lake. There was one more thing she had to do before we entered the all-night party.

"Evangeline," I whisper.

"Come join me, Carter."

She steps out of her jeans and turns to walk toward the water, seductively pulling her panties down her legs.

My body has a mind of its own, and my arms pull my shirt over my head as I start to walk in her direction. It's been four months since we started dating, and just when I think she can't push my limits anymore, she pulls something like this.

Skinny dipping? Me?

Never in a million years would I have thought I'd be doing this here with a girl like her. Yet, here I am. And not with any girl, but the one I've had a crush on since I was thirteen. And here we are about to swim naked in the lake I grew up playing around in.

How'd I get so lucky?

Fuck, even though I hate to admit it, he's right. I just can't imagine feeling that way about another girl. Every few months something reminds me of her, and I get in a funk I can't get out of. This time it was the stupid Facebook post.

I haven't gotten that throwback Thursday picture out of my mind, so I messaged Kaitlyn to see if she had found her. When she said she had, I almost lost my shit. She went to her Facebook account to give me more info only to see that her account was deleted. She said the account was bare. There was no mention of where she was, and even though she accepted her friend request, she hadn't answered any messages or posts beside their first interaction asking if it was actually her. She said yes then went silent again.

She did tell me she changed her name to Angie Smith, which at first gave me so much hope until I realized just how common that name actually is. Not knowing where she's located, I feel like I'm looking for a needle in a haystack, but I'm up for the task and have already ruled out two states.

"Look. I know you feel like you were fucked over and that you still love her and shit, but fuck, bro, it's been years. You have to move on at some point," Cole breaks me from my thoughts.

"You'll never understand," I say through the pillow.

"You're right, I won't. It's time to move on, though."

I turn to give him a look that reinforces my previous statement, and he laughs, making me want to punch him across his glasses ridden face.

"I'd say you need to get laid, but I know firsthand that's not the case. So what's up?"

Cole has become a good friend of mine this past year, but he doesn't get it. He knows a little about her, but not everything. He's never had a serious relationship, and I doubt he ever will.

"Shit, man." He grabs the pillow from me, throwing it to the other couch when I don't respond. "You need to blow some steam, bad. Why don't you try to find someone outside of the club? Take a break from there for a little while. I can't believe I'm even going to suggest this, but maybe you need an actual relationship to rid your memory of this chick."

"You know I don't roll like that." I haven't had a girlfriend in years, and I don't hook up outside of the club. I sit up, taking a deep breath, trying to rid myself of my mood.

"You'd be speaking a different tune if you saw this little hottie in my night class."

"Cole, you know you can't fuck your students. Besides, what are they? Barely eighteen?"

"Not this one, man. She's twenty-eight and smoking hot. She's into me, too. Hasn't even tried to hide it."

"Just don't get yourself into trouble, again. You're lucky you didn't get nailed for that undergrad a few years ago."

"Hey, how was I supposed to know she was only seventeen? There should be a law that says you can't enter college until you're at least legal. That's just false advertising."

I shake my head at his antics. The guy's a manwhore and tries to get at everything that walks. I take advantage at the club, but in everyday life, he's on his own.

"Shut up already about which girl you're going to bang next."

"But where's the fun in that?"

"Just get out," I huff.

"Whatever, Carter. Get your shit in gear. It's pathetic seeing you like this over some chick."

He walks out of my apartment, and I don't take his advice. Instead, I hit the arrow again on my stereo, playing *Falling Inside the Black* on repeat until I get a text from work because I'm the doctor on call.

I debated even going tonight, especially after the shit with Cole today. The need for a release won me over, though. My chest tightens at the thought when I pull my mask over my face and walk down the alley heading toward Club Bridge.

Cole is already here, and when I walk to the bar, he approaches, reaching his hand out in our handshake greeting, saying, "We all good?"

I nod, not in the mood for any talking tonight, and he reads me correctly, knowing I get like this sometimes, and turns to order a drink.

I look at the door as a girl with a mask unlike anything else here, covering more of her face than normal, walks in. Her sexy lingerie shows off her tight little body, and the boy short panties hug her ass perfectly, leaving just the right amount hanging out, piquing my interest.

I hit Cole's back to get his attention, tilting my head in her direction before cocking it to the side, showing my interest without having to say a word.

Cole steals a glance before turning back to me and nodding his silent *I'm on it* communication. To both of our surprise, she heads in our direction, and Cole never leaves my side.

"Hi, boys," the mystery woman says as she puts her hand on Cole's chest. She's definitely not shy, which is a plus.

"Hey, sexy," Cole responds while wrapping his arm around her waist. "I'm Maverick. You look like you want to play tonight."

"Maverick?" she teases. "And who's this? Goose?" She points at me.

I let out a sharp laugh, always teasing him about his name, but he loved that damn movie and wouldn't dare change it for anything…no matter how much he's mocked.

"You'd like that, wouldn't you?" he taunts back.

"Um, no, don't you remember? He dies in the end."

"Why would you care who dies or not? Isn't that the reason you're here, to not care who we really are and what really happens to us?" She tilts her head, letting his reasoning set in, but he continues before she can respond, "You're new here, aren't you?"

She nods while squeezing between us to get the bartender's attention. "A Dirty Shirley, please."

Cole smirks. "That sounds fitting. Are you a dirty girl?"

"Oh, please. Did you really just ask me that?" She looks in my direction. "You gonna let this guy do all the talking? Because he's not doing so well. Maybe it's time you step in."

I smirk at her but don't say a word. I like this chick. It's rare that someone gives Cole shit. Something about her is throwing me, though, and with the mood I'm already in, I think it's best I stay silent for now.

"You think I couldn't bend you over and fuck you right here?" Yup, there's the Cole I truly know.

"Hmmm…Did I hit a nerve, Maverick?" she teases, trying to look innocent in her barely-there lingerie.

Her hand lands on my chest, sending chills running down my spine as she moves slowly, wrapping around my waist and pulling me into her. "Maybe I just want the silent type tonight."

Flowers mixed with ginger invade my senses, making my head spin. I know that smell. It's haunted me for years. Shit, I even bought a bottle just to torture myself and smell it when I'm really fucked up in my head to punish myself for my choices.

She faces me, but her mask covers so much of her face that I can't focus or get my bearings before Cole swiftly turns her around. Pulling her into him, he gives me a moment to breathe.

I watch as he wraps her blond hair around his hands and slightly yanks her head down and to the right, placing kisses on her neck. My eyes squint as features start to come to light, and I shake my head, pushing any ideas to the side.

My mind is really playing tricks on me.

Fingers start to make their way across my leg, and when her hand wraps around my semi hard cock my heart pounds in a way I can't even start to explain. Ever since I saw that photo, I've been thinking I see her everywhere, and this chick is about to push me over the edge.

I grip her hand, ready to yank it away and leave before I lose my shit altogether.

Before I get the chance, Cole stops his little game, saying, "See, you want this. Both of us. Why don't you tell me your name, sweetheart, so I know what to whisper in your ear when I'm fucking you deeply?"

"I'm Evangeline," she says so nonchalantly that I feel the bile run up my throat and burn like a spark of fire.

There's no fucking way.

"Well, that's a pretty name," Cole carries on, not having a clue that my world just stopped spinning and is about to fly off its axis.

Cole may know a lot about my ex, but I've never told him her name. Any mention of it was too much for me to handle, so he lovingly referred to her as Satan due to all the pain she caused me. I'd laugh at the irony of it all because she was anything but. His little nickname would help calm me down, so I let it be.

"Not much of a code name, though. Care to explain your choice?" he asks.

"Let's just say it reminded me of someone I loved once upon a time," she purrs out as she wraps her arms around his neck, pulling away from me.

Feelings of light-headedness rattle through me as thoughts fly around. All these years, all these fucking years! How long I've searched for answers, for the truth, and she just shows up one night at my club, in my city. Just like that.

I've thought so many times of what I'd do if I ever found her. Now that she's here, right in front of me, I'm speechless. Like all these years were a blip, and I've never thought of what to say.

39

Now she wants to fuck my friend. Or better yet, me, having no clue who I really am. I can't. Not now. Maybe not ever. I need to get my shit right first.

I turn to leave, and Cole grabs my shirt, stopping me in my tracks. "Where are you going?"

I look at her, then back at him and shake my head, but before I can turn around, her hand is on my arm.

"I didn't mean to scare you away."

My eyes glance down to where her hand sits, feeling like it's blazing a hole through my skin, but I don't have the strength to pull away. Instead, I tuck my other hand in my pants pocket, hiding my tattoo from her.

"Don't mind him. He's been cranky all week," Cole spits out, obviously done with my shit and ready for me to leave.

"Maybe we can change that mood of yours?" she says as she slides her fingers tightly around my arm, tugging me back to where they both stand. Once I'm there, I release from her grip, tucking my hand away once more.

She's always had this control over me, and I'm learning quickly that some things never change. I couldn't walk away then, and I can't now.

I'm not ready to reveal my cards yet, though. I know most people would want to scream at the top of their lungs, grab her by her shoulders and demand to know why, but something is stopping me.

I can't walk away, but a bigger part of me doesn't want her to know who I am yet. A lot has happened, not just physically but mentally. I'm a completely different person than I was back then, and a small part of me is dying to know how much she's changed too before she pushes me away again.

Because I know she will when she finds out.

I walk back into their circle and watch her hand as she lays it on my chest before looking back into her eyes. Searching to see if the Evangeline I knew then is the same one I'm staring at now.

"Do I get to know your name?" she asks while running her fingers lower on my chest and tugging slightly on the top of my pants.

I shake my head but don't say a word.

"This is—" I abruptly shoot my head over to Cole, stopping his words with my stare.

He can't say my name. She'll know, instantly. I go by Warroad. It's actually the small town I grew up in. That she grew up in. Thousands of miles away from here.

I can tell by his body language that he's confused, but thankfully he's used to my weird moods and brushes it off.

"He wants to play mute, mystery guy tonight, I guess, but don't worry, we'll still show you a good time," Cole says, pulling her away from me and bringing all of her attention back to him.

"I have no doubt about that. I've never done this before." She looks back at me, grabbing my hand. "Will you show me how this is done?" Her innocence almost makes me want to laugh. I know she's far from, but she's playing the part convincingly, and Cole is eating up every second.

Before I know it, the three of us are walking to a corner room, one that gives us a little more privacy and pretty much guarantees no one else will enter our scene.

Cole wastes no time and starts in quickly removing his clothes while kissing his way down her neck. Instead of joining them, I stand back, observing her and the two of them together.

I still can't wrap my head around the fact that she's here. But more importantly, I can't figure out how I feel about it. Watching his hands on her is killing me, but I can't tell if it's jealousy because I don't want him touching her, or because I want it to be my hands caressing her instead.

I know every inch of that body, every curve, the soft plump of her breasts or the tightness of her little ass. It was all mine at one time. I guess it could be mine again. Though she wouldn't know it's me.

Or would she?

She turns in Cole's arms and reaches out to me, grabbing hold of my shirt and pulling me into her, but I resist. My hand covers hers and chills instantly run down my spine. Taking a deep breath, I remove her hand from my belt and shake my head. Stepping back slightly, I lean against a couch, folding my arms over my chest and crossing my legs at my ankles.

I've been a member of this club for a little over a year, and I've never sat back to watch a scene unfold. I may not know if I want to be involved in this threesome, but the idea of watching just made my heart beat a little faster.

Cole notices my retreat from the scene and takes full advantage, getting Evangeline all to himself. His greedy hands pull on her lingerie, removing her bra and springing her breasts free, grabbing one roughly.

That brings her attention off of me, and I chuckle to myself when I watch him pull her nipple between his fingers. She hates her nipples being played with, and my intuition is confirmed when she pulls his fingers away and cups his hands on the bottom of one breast. She may hate her nipples being touched, but she loves having her entire breast played with.

The thought that some things haven't changed makes me smirk and shake my head slightly in amusement.

Cole makes his way down her body, sticking his face directly between her thighs as he pulls her panties down her legs. Watching her body react to being licked makes my dick twitch. It's the way her head falls back, making her long, blond hair flow down her back as she grips Cole's hair for dear life.

Suddenly I'm fifteen again, lusting over the girl who just appeared from under the water with her head tilted back, allowing the water to flow down her wet body. Nothing has changed yet everything has. And my cock responds in the exact same way. Only now, it's worse. I've been inside her. I've felt what it is to have her clench around me in the most delicious way.

My head fights with my body as I slide down onto the couch, sitting on the edge, bringing my hands up to a steeple on my knees, and placing the tips of my fingers at my lips. A low growl releases from my mouth as I push every ounce of air out of my lungs, trying not to blink my eyes, so I don't miss a second.

My lust catches her attention and she looks at me, tilting her head slightly to the side before running her hand up her waist, cupping her breast, looking directly at me. She's putting on a show, trying to tempt me to join their scene, having no clue why I'm sitting here, completely lost in her and losing my fucking mind.

Without each of us paying attention, Cole stands up, removing his pants and walking behind her. He must notice my enjoyment of watching the two of them—and being the amazing friend he is—he not only doesn't get between us, he positions her perfectly so I can get mine while he gets his.

Fingers appear from between her legs as he works his way in, teasing and testing her limits, making sure she's ready for him. Her body falls in response, giving him complete control as she goes limp in his arms.

I can't hear what is said, but Cole whispers something in her ear, and both of them stare directly at me while he enters her from behind slowly. Her body tenses and then rolls in response to him pushing his way in and standing completely still, never taking their eyes off of me.

I nod my response, feeling like I need to give my approval for them to continue. Once I do, Cole responds by wrapping one arm around her shoulders, the other on her waist, bracing her while he pulls out and slams back in.

A deep moan spills from her lips and her hands reach out, one holding on to his arm and the other gripping his other hand like she's holding on for dear life. But never once removing her stare from me.

She's getting off on the fact that I'm watching her get fucked from behind, and suddenly, this scene went in a different direction.

Sitting further back on the couch, I fold my leg over my knee, placing my right arm on the armrest, and run my finger over my lips. When I open them slightly, she does the same. When I stick my finger in my mouth, her finger moves to hers and does the same.

She's in a trance while Cole fucks her from behind, but my control is the one she wants. My heart pounds. My stomach aches. I want her. I need her. I've never been so fucked up in my life.

I walk up, placing my hand on her face and—fuck me—the sensation that runs through my body is too much when her head leans into my touch.

My heart can't do this.

Instead, I lean in, whispering to Cole, "Fuck her good," and walk away, leaving the club before I do something I'll regret.

Chapter 10

CARTER
10 YEARS EARLIER

"So we're drawing the line?"

"Carter, we have to. Your parents are right. I'd just be a distraction."

"Screw my parents. I still can't believe my mom said those awful things to you."

I've never known my mom to be anything but the sweetest woman alive, but the other day, when we tried to talk to them about her coming with me to L.A., I saw someone I never knew existed. She threw out so many nasty insults about Evangeline. Calling her a gold digger, trailer trash, and the worst part, a whore. I grabbed Evangeline's hand and stormed out of their house.

At that moment, I was ready to give everything up for Evangeline, my scholarship, Los Angeles, my dreams. All of it. But now, here we stand, a week later, and I leave tomorrow night.

"Don't be mad at her. They just want a better life for you. They don't want you to stay here, working at the mill for the rest of your life. You have this amazing opportunity that you worked so hard for."

"But we can make it work."

"How? I don't have any money. You know my parents don't either. You have a scholarship with living expenses included. I couldn't find a job that quickly to pay for a down payment and rent. Remember, a studio apartment out there was ridiculous."

"I can find a part-time job to help you pay your rent."

"No, Carter. I won't let you do that. I don't want anything to come between you and your dreams, especially me."

"But you *are* my dreams."

"And you're mine. So go get your awesome doctor degree and then we'll never have to worry about money so we can live our dreams. Till then, I'll work, save up as much as I can and hopefully, one day, I can come join you."

"But what about you till then?"

"What about me? I'll be fine. Come on, really? Where am I gonna go?" She pauses like she just had the best idea ever then starts to jump up and down. "Let's do something crazy tonight. Just you and me."

"What kind of crazy are you thinking about?" I eye her up and down sexually.

"Well, yes, that kind," she says, but I interrupt her when I lean down, breaking up her words to steal a kiss. "We'll definitely do that, but I had something else in mind."

"Okay, like what?" I say, and her smile turns so bright it almost brings me to my knees. That's what I love about her. She's always thinking up unique ideas, and I want like hell to bring her with me. If only I could.

"Let's get tattoos. Something small. Something stupid…that only we know the meaning of."

I grin. "Didn't think this would go that route, but fuck it. What you got in mind?"

She pushes her lips together in thought. "Let's see, something to do with drawing the line. Not saying goodbye just—"

"So we get a line," I interrupt her.

"Huh?" She squints her eyes, confused by my suggestion.

"Yeah, we get a straight line, um…" I grab her hand and turn it over. "Right here across the inside of our wrists."

"Really?"

I can tell she's on the fence, but I'm starting to really dig the idea. "Yeah, that way it won't be noticeable to everyone else, but to me and you, it will mean the world. Constantly reminding us if we're patient we'll be able to cross the line someday."

Her arms wrap around my neck. "Exactly! That's the exact meaning I was hoping for."

"I told you. I get you. You're my kind of crazy." I kiss her lips before smacking her ass. "Let's go, the closest tattoo shop has to be an hour away."

And it was. An hour and twenty minutes to be exact, but the time flew by. We were all in, and with this being our last night together, nothing was going to stop us. The tattoo artist laughed at our idea, but we didn't explain the meaning. No one needs to know but us.

I leave tomorrow, and I know both of our parents are going to flip their lids, but we don't care. Instead of going home when we pulled back into town, we found a spot by the lake, laid out a blanket, and spent the night lost in each other.

For one last night, one last kiss, one last love, I gave her my all. My everything. I pray that the love we shared tonight will be enough. Enough for her to wait for me because I know there's no way I could ever live without her. I just need to make it through what's ahead of me. My scholarship only pays for me to be in the dorms. So until then, I'll study my ass off so I can get my degree to one day be able to afford for her to come to Los Angeles with me.

Every day away from her has been hard, but I'm trying to see the bigger picture and my end goal through all of this. I tend to stare at my tattoo for probably longer than I should, but right now, it's the only thing getting me through the day.

It's been a month since I left. We spoke daily at first, multiple times a day actually, but it was killing us both. Anytime I heard her voice it would take every ounce of my control not to quit school and fly back home just to be with her.

I made the mistake of telling her one lonely night, and ever since then, she cut me off, saying we needed to cut the cord, really draw the line and separate from each other completely. I fought it, but deep down I knew it was what needed to happen. Doesn't mean it makes it any easier, though.

Chris, my dorm roommate, is finally dragging my ass out for the night. He knows all about Evangeline and keeps reminding me it's time to live again. I'm afraid I don't know how.

He's a sophomore, so he's already a member of a fraternity and brings me along to hang out at their frat house. When we walk in, wall-to-wall bodies bounce in the air as loud music thumps through my ears, bringing my senses to life. Every corner I turn there are ten more girls dancing provocatively with each other and putting on a show for every guy to enjoy.

"What's up, bro?" A guy walks up to Chris, slapping his hand in the air and looking in my direction. "Who's this guy?"

"What up, Sean? This is Carter, my roommate."

"Hey." I nod.

"Any friend of Chris' is welcome in this house. Let me get you a beer."

Two seconds later, I'm handed a red solo cup as Sean is pulled onto the makeshift dance floor in the middle of what I assume to be their dining room.

Someone calls Chris from the kitchen and before he leaves he looks over at me, asking, "You good?"

I nod just as a pretty blonde with short shorts and an even shorter top walks up and answers for me, "Yeah, he's good."

I smirk, still not sure if I want this attention or not. I look her up and down with a slight tilt pulling on my lips the farther down my eyes travel. When they meet with her eyes again, I bring my beer to my lips, swallowing the pain I feel inside and trying to move on one step at a time.

"I'm Lucy," she says close to my ear so I can hear her over the music, but I know by the way she pushes her chest out, it was to show off her body more than anything else.

"Carter," is all I respond before I feel my phone vibrate in my pocket. When I glance down, I see an eight-hundred number, so I silence it, having no idea why an eight-hundred number would be calling me right now. I wouldn't be able to hear the person anyway with the music blasting, so I slide it back into my pocket.

"You're new here, aren't you?" Lucy asks.

"Yup, how about you?"

"I'm a Junior. Psyche major, halfway there, thank God," she over embellishes.

"Well, I'm on the first leg of med school, so I won't be saying that for a long time."

"Oh." She comes up close, leaving no room in between my body and hers. "You want to be a doctor, huh?"

"That's the goal," I say, trying to pull away a little from her by bringing my beer up to my lips. I know I need to move on but not like this. Not this fast.

Her friend walks up right as my phone rings again. I pull it out of my pocket right as she pulls it from my hands, noticing the eight-hundred number as well.

She answers, "Sorry, there's nothing you can sell this hottie tonight. He's already got his hands full with Lucy and me." She laughs, hanging up the phone and handing it back to me. "I thought sales calls aren't allowed to call your cell phone?" she questions, and I agree with her statement.

They both stay and talk to me for a while, but I try to make sure they know I'm not interested, at least not right now. More friends come and join in on our conversation, and instantly my nerves relax. The group atmosphere gives me some relief so I can get my feet wet before jumping in completely.

The beers flow more easily as the night progresses, and I get to know a few different guys and even more girls. Every single one of them shows a little more interest when they realize I'm pre-med, which instantly puts up even more red flags. People warned me, but it's shocking to see there really are gold diggers who just want to bag a doctor.

At two in the morning, Chris and I stumble back to our dorm; him with a female on his arm and me knowing it's going to be a long night. I could have had my pick of a few girls, but there was no way I was going to have a one-night fling when my heart was still back home.

Instead, I head to the student lounge where I crash on the couch, waiting for the all-clear to be allowed back in my room. I don't hold out hope, though.

I wake up with the worst kink in my neck and an even bigger pounding in my head. I can't believe he left me to sleep on this couch all night. We need to set up some parameters for what's cool and what's not for having the room to ourselves. This was definitely not cool.

I grab my phone to check the time and see I have a voicemail from the eight-hundred number last night. Leaning my head back against the headrest of the couch, I let out a long sigh as I bring the phone up to my ear.

"Carter…Fuck, Carter, where are you?"

It's Evangeline, and suddenly my heart is beating like a bass drum with the night's pain forgotten as I sit up, listening more intently.

"There's been an accident. My parents…" she trails off, and I can hear her sobbing through the phone. "I left home without my phone. I'm calling from a payphone in the hospital. I didn't know who else to call. God…" She pauses. "Where are you?"

She hangs up, and when I look down at my phone, I see I have eleven missed calls starting from around the time we entered the party. Only one message, though, left the first time she called. Memories of the girl last night answering my phone makes the left-over alcohol creep up a little too high in my stomach, and I have to fight the urge to hurl.

How could I have let that happen? She needed me, and I ignored the call. I wasn't there for her.

I click her name as quickly as I can and wait, but it goes straight to voicemail. After leaving a message, I call my parents.

"Mom, what happened? I got a call from Evan—"

Before I can finish my mom cries into the phone. "Oh, honey, there's been an accident. I don't know what happened."

"Is everyone okay?"

She cries into the phone, "No, baby. Sandy and Dave, they, oh my God—"

She can't even say it.

She doesn't need to.

Evangeline's parents were killed last night in an accident, and I ignored her call.

Chapter 11

EVANGELINE
PRESENT DAY

There was no way I could hide the smile on my face from my first night at the club. I wish Kamii was at work when I walked in, but the reality of why she wasn't there being all too real of a reminder to bring me back to my life. The good and the bad.

The morning goes on when my cell rings, and I notice Kamii's face appearing on my screen. "What's up, girl? How's mommy hood treating you?"

"I'm so in love. I haven't slept much, but I try to rest when she's napping," she responds with happiness lacing her tone right before she yawns.

"Why did you call my cell instead of the office line?"

"Hello…?" she squeals into the phone. "I know it's almost ten-thirty and time for you to take a break, so get your little bootie up, step outside, and tell me about last night!" she demands.

I let out a loud laugh before clicking a few things on my computer and pushing my chair away from my desk. "Oh, *now* you want to know all about my sex life?" I tease her. I've always told her everything even though I knew it made her uncomfortable. But of course, she's never actually asked for the low-down, dirty details.

"Stop, you know this is different."

"Yeah, because it has nothing to do with love and everything to do with fucking." I stop when I hear her gasp. "You surprise me at every turn. I only wish I knew this side of you sooner."

"Yeah, yeah, yeah, just tell me. How did it go?"

"Nothing like I expected but everything I dreamed of."

"What exactly did you expect?"

"Remember I wanted to hook up with the two guys?"

"Were they not there?"

"Oh no, they were there. But one of them was very cryptic. He wouldn't talk, and I never got his name."

"That's Maverick and—"

"No. Don't tell me. I don't want to know. That's what made it so hot. He never even touched me. He watched the entire time, giving us his permission it almost seemed and then he up and left before it was over."

"Are you serious? I've never seen him turn down a good time."

"That's the thing. It still was an amazing time, and he was getting off as much as we were by just watching. It was such an unreal feeling to feel Maverick's cock—"

"Okay, that's enough," she interrupts, making me grin. "I may be more open about sex, but I still can't talk about it like that."

"Well, you asked." I chuckle. "Just know it was hot. I hope he continues this little game of his."

"I'm glad you had fun. Enjoy yourself there." She pauses. "What am I talking about? Of course you'll enjoy yourself."

"You know it, girl," I snap back.

"So any other issues? Everything seems pretty calm and like a good crowd was there?"

"Yeah, I noticed a few people I didn't see my first time, but I'm paying attention, trying to recognize who's around."

"I know we don't really need you to do anything. It's just nice to know we have someone kind of undercover while we're gone."

"I feel so James Bondish with my assignment. Give that beautiful baby girl a kiss for me. I've got to get back up there before my bitch of a boss hunts me down. I swear she's the worst."

"Ha. Ha. Ha," she slowly jokes through the line. "Enjoy the rest of your day."

"You too."

It's a good thing I have class tonight. I'm more than tempted to make an appearance at the club, but then I remember it's BDSM night, so that helps squash the burning itch deep in my stomach. I can wait until tomorrow.

I think.

Thankfully, Kamii was able to find someone to help on Friday nights, so I don't have to worry about not being there for them either.

Instead, I head out for my class. With Kamii gone, I was able to get off early, so I went home to change into my black leggings and Ugg boots along with an oversized shirt that hangs slightly off my shoulder when it's not evenly distributed on my body. Add with my hair pulled back into a ponytail, I'm definitely going for the super comfy look tonight.

Everyone has chosen to sit in the same seats each class, so no matter how early or late I am, I still get my chair up front. Not only am I eager to learn, but I'm not going to lie, I like staring at my teacher's ass when he writes on the board.

As I walk up to my desk, Professor Spence's glare doesn't hide a thing when he eyes me up and down. The small smile that pulls on his lips tells me he doesn't mind my casual attire one bit. In fact, he almost looks appreciative of it.

"Nice to see you, Miss Smith," Professor Spence basically slurs the words with his eyes not meeting mine until I stop walking.

"Professor Spence," is all I reply before I wink and sit.

His head tilts down, shaking slightly as he hides the laughter coming from his lips before standing up to greet the class. "Can someone give me the definition of morals?"

After a brief moment of silence, a voice speaks up, obviously reading from their phone, "A lesson, especially one concerning what is right or prudent, that can be derived from a story, a piece of information, or an experience."

He squints his eye and pinches his lips to the side, showing that wasn't exactly the answer he wanted.

The same person keeps going, "Or, a person's standards of behavior or beliefs concerning what is and is not acceptable for them to do."

"Yes." He snaps his fingers, pointing to the student. "Behavior or beliefs of what is not acceptable. What exactly does that mean?"

Someone else pipes in, "It's what's right or wrong."

"Ah, but who is to decide what's right or wrong?" he asks.

"The law," Alex yells from a few rows back.

"Well, yes and no. Angie, can I use you as my model?" He holds out his hand to me like he's going to help me stand up. I take it but drop it quickly after I stand next to him before he continues. "I just held her hand, be it for a quick second, but could that be considered morally wrong?"

"I guess it depends on where you are or what the context of said hand-holding was?"

"Exactly." He pauses and comes closer, placing his arm around my shoulder, giving me a side hug like a friend would. "And what about this?"

"It depends on who you are to each other," Charlie shouts out.

"True. If we were friends, this would be totally normal. But say, as her teacher, or her boss, what would it be?"

"That depends on your relationship. It could be okay, and it could be wrong."

"Yes, this would be considered the gray area. But think about that word again. Morals. To some, this would be considered wrong where to others it would be acceptable. It depends on what your morals are when it comes to this exact topic. So what if I did this?" He comes up behind me, putting his hands on my hips.

To the class, it looks somewhat innocent, but the way his groin pushes into me while pulling me back into him proves to me it's anything but.

"That would be crossing the line, legally and morally," Charlie shouts and by his tone, I think he noticed what was really going on.

Professor Spence leans in to my ear and whispers, "Busted," before stepping back and acting like nothing happened, addressing the class as he walked back to the board. "And there it is. Today we're going to discuss the difference between legal duty versus moral duty."

As I walk back to my desk, my head is stuck high in a cloud but not because of what he just did but the way his voice tickled my neck as he whispered only to me, from behind, reminding me of—

No fucking way.

Chapter 12

EVANGELINE

I stared at Professor Spence for the rest of the class last night. Not listening to a thing he said but more trying to figure him out. Paying attention to his body, listening to his voice, anything to show me if this is Maverick. There are definitely some similarities; his size and skin tone are similar to what I remember, but it is very dimly lit in the club.

His jaw line along with his voice could definitely match. But I've only been in the club one time, so tonight I need to pay very close attention.

I'm fighting with my curiosity of knowing and my fun of not knowing. The excitement of the club is not knowing who this person is. Now that I might know, I didn't want it to ruin the anonymity of the club for me. The thought of it turning into just another one-night-stand type of thing bothered me. I just joined. I'm afraid if I know who he is then it will ruin everything, and I'll be left with only the one night of fun I had.

And what are the freaking odds of me joining a sex club—finally—and I fuck my teacher. Surely, the world isn't conspiring against me that much.

It's that damn question; did curiosity really kill the cat, or in my case, my pussy?

As I enter the club, still having no clue what I want to do or not do, I decide, fuck it, I'm going to pray I'm wrong and that it's not him. If it is by chance my professor, at least it will make my class that much more interesting.

I look around, noticing people already starting to scene, and the sight alone sends tingles down my legs and a rush of excitement through my veins. I pause, deciding to sit and watch the foursome unfolding in front of me.

I'm here to keep an eye on things for Preston and Kamii, so what better scene than a foursome. I still can't believe I get to be a part of something like this, and I'll be damned if I'm not going to sit and watch, or rather, enjoy my view.

To my surprise, I feel a warm arm wrap around my waist, pulling me into him and whispering close to my ear, "Busted."

Professor Spence.

I turn around to face him. "Excuse me, what's that supposed to mean?" *Does he know, too?*

"Hey…" He pulls me into his front. "Don't be ashamed. There's nothing wrong with enjoying watching people fuck."

I try to look past his mask and into his eyes, but I can barely make out the dark orbs looking back at me. Before I respond, I take my time, looking him up and down, studying his body, his clothing, even his shoes. Trying to find anything to accurately identify him.

I have my suspicions, but I'm not ready to state the fact yet, so I decide to play along. "Where's your friend?"

"You liked that, didn't you? The way he watched me fuck you last time."

"Maybe," I say, placing my hand on his chest.

"He's here. Don't you worry. You want to play with us again, tonight?"

"Is that even a question?"

"Well…" He leans in and kisses up my neck. "You liked me that much then, huh?"

"Don't be so sure of yourself. Your friend had a lot to do with it, too," I tease.

"Ha." He laughs out. "Let's go find him then, your highness."

He takes my hand and walks me to his friend, who's leaning against the bar, and to my surprise, he's wearing a different mask than the last time I saw him. This one is bigger, covering more of his face, making him appear even more secretive. His mood doesn't look as bothered tonight, but he's still standoffish with his body language. A part of me is dying to know why, but a different part is praying he plays the same game.

He looks delicious in designer jeans and a tight Henley that's showing off the crazy muscles this man has. He nods at my arrival as he brings his beer to his lips, taking a drink while his eyes roam up and down the length of my body. I do the same and am stopped short when I notice a thick watch on his wrist. It's unlike one I've ever seen before where the band is more of a cuff and is a good two inches thick. I took him for a business type, maybe a lawyer like Cole, but this watch makes me think he's more of a punk or skater.

Interesting.

"Do I get to know your name tonight?"

He doesn't respond, just shakes his head, and fuck me, my whole body sings with excitement knowing I'll get another night like the last.

"Then what's your plan? Are we going to play a game?" I tease, stepping up to him, plastering my body with his. He doesn't push me away, and for a brief moment, his hand grips my waist tightly, almost too tight, before turning me to the side to face Maverick as he brings the bottle to his lips again.

Rejection starts to fight its way into my mind, but it's quickly pushed away when his hand reaches up, moving my hair to the side like he's admiring what he sees. His hand stays there for a few breaths before nodding his head to Maverick like he's ready to go.

Maverick guides me to the same room, and my secret man sits in his same spot. I think we're going the same route when a deep, husky voice calls from in front of me. "You want to play a game, so let's play a game."

I look up, and the man is sitting with a slight smirk on his face as he leans forward, resting his elbows on his knees and circling a beer bottle down low between his fingertips.

Something about him intrigues me. His mystery. His demeanor. His everything.

I hear Maverick chuckle, and I respond, "What do you have in mind?"

"I'm in charge tonight. You. Do. What. I. Say," he says all long and drawn out but keeping in his deep voice that reminds me of Batman and Bruce Wayne. It's obvious this isn't his real voice, and a part of me is dying to know why he's going to such extreme lengths to conceal his identity. But the other part of me almost wants to jump for joy at the thought of not knowing and playing his little charade.

"What's the fun in that for me?" I taunt.

Maverick grabs my arm, pulling me into him. "Dare you doubt us?"

Chills rush down my spine, the fear of the unknown sending my blood rushing through my veins as my heart beats what feels like a mile a minute.

"Never," I whisper as Maverick's hands reach up, cupping my breasts roughly at the same time, which only adds to my excitement. And fear.

"Good answer," he whispers in my ear before he pushes me back against the bed.

I'm almost positive this is Professor Spence...Cole...my teacher...so if they want to play a game, I'll play right along with them. I'll let them think they're in control, but at least for right now, I have the true upper hand.

"Strip," Maverick demands.

"You didn't say Simon says," I taunt back while gripping my hands behind my back, pushing my breast up on display as I swing lightly back and forth.

His lips pull up to a smirk, and I know he likes the push and pull, yet another thing confirming this is truly him.

"Okay, Simon says take off your clothes."

I grin, reaching behind me to unhook my bra. I guess I have to because he said Simon says.

I hold it up to him, dangling it on one finger as I sit on the bed on my knees. "Do you want it?" I ask.

"Give it here," Secret grunts out.

Both Maverick and I turn to him. For a second I forgot he was even here. Watching.

I fling my bra his way, and he catches it with ease, running it through his fingers and thoroughly examining it before looking back at me.

"You lose. I didn't say Simon says," he taunts when our eyes lock.

He stuffs it into his suit pocket before sitting back, taking another swig of his beer and giving us a nod to continue.

"Simon says undo my shirt," Maverick commands, bringing the attention back to him.

My lips tilt up as I crawl over to where he's standing and slowly start to undo each button, leaning in to kiss every spot I reveal, one inch at a time.

"Simon didn't say kiss me," Maverick points out, placing his finger under my chin and tilting it up to bring his lips to mine for a brief moment. "Who's in control here?"

Secret speaks up in his same harsh voice, "I am."

Every time he talks, shivers tingle down my spine. The mystery he's holding makes me more excited, and when Maverick wraps his hand around my pussy, feeling the wetness seep through, he leans down to kiss me again.

"Should I be jealous?" he whispers into my ear. "Why do I get the feeling you like him more than me?"

I turn my attention to him. "Maybe I do." I tilt my head to the side, giving him a sexy smile.

"But he hasn't even touched you. I'm the one who made you cum last time."

He leans down, roughly pulling my panties off while pushing me back on the bed to remove them completely.

When he climbs on top of me, I giggle. "Do I sense some jealousy?"

"I'm the one about to fuck you. There's nothing I have to be jealous of."

I sneak a peek over at Secret, but he's gone. I jump slightly when I hear, "Sit up," in a deep, demanding voice to my side.

"I knew he couldn't stay away for long," Maverick teases, sliding back, giving him room to sit behind me.

He's removed his jacket, but his shirt and pants are still on. My hand reaches over to his chest, wanting to remove it, but he stops me. Without saying a word, he shakes his head and moves my hand back to Maverick's shirt to continue undressing him.

I look back at him, and he nods, nudging me to finish the job as he sits behind me.

Maverick helps me remove his shirt, and his pants are quick to follow.

"Your lips," Secret whispers out. "Wrap them around his cock."

Though I'm being told what to do, I've already decided two can play this game, and it's about to be on Mr. Secret man.

Instead of just leaning forward, where I easily could have reached out to grab Maverick, I reposition myself. Crawling on all fours, I push Maverick backward a little, giving myself room to give Secret the perfect view. Taunting him in the best way I know how.

With my ass.

I hear his groan when I'm close enough to him that I know he can see my glistening pussy almost dripping at this point. I look over my shoulder, trying to catch a glimpse of him before I wrap my hand around Maverick.

Through my legs, I can see his hand move up then down, then up again. He's tempted to touch me, to run his fingers through my slit, and I love that I have the power once again.

Like I ever lost it.

A quiet laugh slips through my lips before I wrap them around Maverick, taking him in fully before pulling him back out and swiping my tongue around his tip.

His hands reach up to wrap in my hair and pull me in closer. I fight the urge, trying to keep control, and instead, pull back completely and suck his balls into my mouth. The movement shocks him, and he gives in instantly.

"Maverick," I hear Secret grunt out.

He can tell I'm taking control and knows he has met his match at this little game.

"Fuck, she's licking my balls, though," Maverick bites out while he holds my head there. "Simon says don't stop."

I grin, pulling back, knowing if I stay now they're in control again.

Secret reaches up to pull me back into him. It's the closest I've been to him, and the thought sends a warmth through my body that I haven't felt in years, taking me by surprise. I try to sit up, but he holds me there.

Harshly whispering in my ear, "No more Simon says. Don't try to take control. That's our job."

I turn to look at my secret guy behind me but am caught off guard when the feeling of wet heat licks up my pussy, and my head drops back, not expecting the act, but instantly pushing my hands through Maverick's hair.

Maverick's hands grip my hips, pulling me down, away from Secret, and instantly, I miss his warmth behind me. My head tilts back to look for him, reaching my other hand out, trying to pull him down to me.

His hand stops mine mid-movement, of course, shaking his head again and pushing farther away from me. Frustration starts to burn inside; frustration from him and also from Maverick, who has slowed his movements just enough to drive me crazy.

I buck my hips, trying to bring his lips closer, harder, but he pulls back as well and looks up at me, giving me the sexiest smirk I've seen since that first day in class, and I just got my confirmation.

This is definitely my teacher.

The thought lights a fire from deep inside. I wasn't sure if I wanted to know, but now that I do, I want it even more. I want him inside me. I want him to fuck me, and the fact that he doesn't seem to have a clue it's me makes my desire even stronger.

I kick off my silver heels and bring my feet up to Maverick's cock, trying my best to wrap them around and stroke him softly. He moans his approval, so I continue my movements, trying to encase him even more before rubbing the top of my foot over his balls.

He pulls back as he rips open a condom and slips it on with ease before moving up my body, kissing his way through my stomach, my breast, and finally to my lips. His hands reach out, gripping both of mine and pulling them out to each side.

Maverick's body hovers directly over me, but he doesn't enter. Instead, he entangles his tongue with mine, leisurely kissing me while making no move for anything else.

I wrap my legs around him, shifting my hips, trying to move his cock to where I want it. Where I'm dying to have it.

"She's gaining control again," Secret warns from behind me, reminding me he's here.

I can't believe I was so worked up with Maverick that I forgot where I was. Knowing he's been watching this whole time makes me that much hornier.

"Fuck, man. I'm trying, but I need to take her," Maverick whimpers, seemingly about to lose control.

I buck my hips just right, and he can't deny it anymore. I'm soaking wet, and his tip is right where I need it. Pushing myself down on the bed moves him in that much more. Only centimeters are inside me, but I'm about to lose my mind.

His lips never leave mine, and besides tiny little movements in any direction, he's got me completely pinned down.

Breaking his lips from mine, I pant, "Please. Now. Simon fucking says."

I hear them both laugh, but at this point, I don't care who wins our little game. I just want this burn inside of me to be extinguished in the most beautiful way.

Thank God, he finally pushes the rest of the way in, and I explode almost on contact. I scream out my release as Maverick pumps hard, whispering in my ear, "The night has just begun, so you better hold on."

Chapter 13

CARTER

My mind is a wreck, and my heart is a mess.

How can watching who I thought was the love of my life getting fucked by my best friend turn me on more than anything I've ever encountered? I should hate her. I should hate him. But every time I envision last night, my cock twitches to life, begging to be touched.

I've dreamed of what I would say to her, what I'd do if, or when, I ever found her. Yet there she was, right in front of me, and all I could do was walk away. Mainly because all I wanted to do was be with her again. Hold her, run my fingers over her body as I ran kisses down her neck.

I've always enjoyed watching women get off while Cole fucked them, but seeing her brought everything to a whole new level. Something I've never experienced before, but what the fuck? Normal guys don't get off on this shit. I should want her all to myself.

The turmoil I was feeling last night was too much. I moved to her, thinking if I just touched her something would tell me what I should do. But it didn't. The feelings got stronger, more intense. I wanted to be inside her. I wanted to show her what Cole and I could do to her.

But I couldn't. Not now. Her not knowing who I am tore at me, clenching my chest and making my stomach turn until I was forced to walk away from them.

I saw her reach back for me, wanting me to join in, but I was already gone.

Knowing she wanted me there pulled on me even more. To her, though, I'm not me. I'm this big secret, and this is all just a game.

A game I know I'm going to lose.

It's my day off, but I need to clear my mind, so I head over to the hospital. There's something about being there that brings me to my happy place. No matter how shitty I feel about the cards I was dealt, seeing what families and kids are dealing with helps put things in perspective, and by the end of the day, I'm kicking my own ass for any issues I thought I was having.

Since I'm not actually working, I get to hang out with the kids more today. Kyle has been here the longest, and our leaderboard is getting a little lopsided. It's time for me to show him who's really the boss and bring him to the next level.

When I walk in, he's not in the playroom, so I head to his room, where I find him lying in bed. His head is looking out the window, and he turns to me, pain written all over his face.

"What's up, bud?" I say, walking to him and softly rubbing his shoulder.

"Just another day." He tries to smile out.

"You not feeling so good today?" He doesn't respond, rather shakes his head before looking back at the window. "Want me to leave you alone so you can get some rest?"

"Nah, grab a chair. I can't sleep anyway."

I do, pulling up next to him and leaning back. I put my feet on the edge of his bed and fold my arms behind my head.

"Make yourself at home, why don't you," he teases.

"Hey, it's my day off. I'm not going to sit all stiff in this uncomfortable chair while you lie in that cozy bed," I tease, putting my feet down. I lean forward. "So, tell me something, little man."

"I'm not so little, you know," he boasts.

This is what we do. He tries to act much older while I try to make him remember, and more importantly tell him, to enjoy being a kid for as long as he can. Growing up only brings on more responsibilities and heartache.

"Oh really, you a man now?"

"Well, no. But I have a girlfriend." The way his voice lifts when he says girlfriend makes me chuckle.

"Shut up. No, you don't," I badger him, trying to get a rise out.

He sits up slightly. "I do. It's Sophia."

I tilt my head to the side, raising my eyebrows in mock surprise. "Really? Over in room thirty-six? Sure she's not too good for you?"

Even though he's sick, I still mess with him and treat him like other boys would treat him. Getting shit from your friends is part of growing up, and it breaks my heart that Kyle won't ever have that.

"Shut up," he throws back. "I'm doing better than you are. You don't even have a girlfriend."

"What makes you say that?" I'm shocked the story went to me. I think the teacher just got schooled at his own game. I've never been so proud.

"Come on. Isn't it obvious? It's your day off, yet you're here, with me. Where you always are. If you had a girlfriend or any type of life outside this hospital, you wouldn't be here right now."

I sit up slightly offended but try to act more serious than I feel. "I have a life," I defend. "I have friends, well, one friend." I pause. I can't tell him anything else, but mainly because he's a kid, and well, there are just certain things you don't share with anyone.

"See, one friend." He glares his disapproval before giggling. "Na, don't lie, you have two. I'm your friend."

I grin, reaching out for his hand. "That means a lot, bro."

"Yeah, yeah, whatever. But I can't be your girlfriend, too. It's time to man up, *bro*."

I let out a loud laugh. This kid is wise beyond his years, and the way he said bro, mocking me, proves that maybe he knows what he's talking about— like a parent talking to a child.

I lean back in my chair again, putting my feet up and watching his fake annoyance at the gesture before sighing his approval. I take a deep breath, diving into the memory of my past. "I had a girlfriend, at one point…"

TEN YEARS AGO

"Mom, Dad, where are you guys? The mail, it's here. There's a letter from UCLA!" I yell out, running through my house as my fingers tingle from the envelope in my hand, the very *big* envelope.

"Carter, oh my God, open it!" my mom yells as they both come running in from outside, just as excited and nervous as I am.

I've worked my ass off at school, taking every AP class I could, even driving a half hour every night to the next town to take pre-college courses at the local community college to try to compete with other kids from more affluent areas. I need this admission, but more importantly, I need a full scholarship.

My parents are great people, but living in this tiny town doesn't offer much chance for advancement. They have lived paycheck to paycheck most of my life, barely getting by and trying their best to make a great life for me.

I want to make them proud. I want to show them their sacrifice was worth it, and I want to help them the way they helped me.

With trembling fingers, I rip open the envelope, pulling out the stack of papers to read, "Congratulations, we are pleased to inform you that you've been offered a full scholarship to University of California, Los Angeles. Your tuition, lodging, and books are all included…"

I try to read the rest, but my mom's arms wrap around me as she cries into my shoulder, holding me tighter than she has in years. I drop the paper, engulfing her in my arms as my dad wraps around both of us. We all cry tears of joy, tears of relief. I did it. Everything I've worked for, every party I didn't go to, every test I studied my ass off for, every hour I volunteered, every mile I drove to take extra classes has finally paid off.

I'm getting out of here.

Later that night I decided to go out for once, hang out with my friends and celebrate.

"Holy shit, is that Carter Donavon at a party?" James shouts out as I walk up to his truck parked in the middle of a field. He's sitting on the tailgate, and six other trucks are lined up in a similar position with a keg directly in the middle of it all.

My best friend, Alan, answers for me, just as proud of my accomplishment, "We're celebrating. Carter here is getting out of this shit hole, on a full ride to UCLA." He hits my chest, and his beaming smile makes me laugh.

James jumps off the truck. "No shit?" He grabs my hand. "Congrats, man."

"What? What's going on?"

I turn and see her. Evangeline. I've had a crush on her for years but never acted on it. She's so out of my league. She's the popular girl in school, the crazy girl, always doing wild things and causing a commotion in the community.

I've watched her from afar, lusting after her every move. I've heard rumors she has a thing for me, but I never believed them. Or more, I tried not to. I wanted to so badly, but I couldn't let anything get in the way of my dreams, so I kept my head down, focusing on what needed to be done.

"I got in," is all I say as a slight fear runs through my body from just looking at her.

"You're leaving?" I swear I see a bit of sadness in her eyes, and I know it shouldn't, but it excites me to see I affect her that way.

"Yeah, I got into UCLA on a full ride," I say, pride bouncing around me.

"When do you leave?" she asks, walking up closer to me, placing her hand on my chest, and I hope to God she can't feel my heart beating like a bass drum deep in my chest.

"Not till August," I say, taking her cue and throwing caution to the wind. I already got in, so the idea of actually enjoying the rest of my senior year starts to take over, quickly.

I wrap my arms around her waist and bring her into me. I hear my friends laugh, yelling, "Get you some." And then they walk away, leaving us alone.

I look back at them before smirking in her direction. "Don't listen to them," I suggest, hoping deep down that she actually will, in fact, listen to them.

"Hmmm, it's April, so you'll leave in four months, then?" she says, snuggling up even closer.

"Probably not until the end of the month, so more like five months," I whisper, swallowing a lump in my throat.

She looks up at me. Her eyes are so beautiful, so perfect. We stare into each other, acknowledging for the first time there's something between us. I take a chance, leaning down, softly touching my lips to hers, and I'm done for.

This girl is everything.

Chapter 14

EVANGELINE

I walk into class wearing the same silver high heel shoes I had on at the club on Saturday. I want to mess with *Professor Spence* to see if he recognizes me. I thought about it all day Sunday, trying to figure out if I should continue this little game or just come out and say it.

I like games, what can I say?

Without a word, I walk to my chair, sitting down and shuffling through my bag, trying not to pay attention to my teacher.

Ashley pokes me from behind. "I love your shoes. So sassy," she boasts, and I swear I want to kiss her right now.

I lift my shoes, showing them off even more. "Aren't they? I've had some good times in these shoes lately."

When I turn back around, I see Cole looking at me, but I can't tell if it's my shoes or my legs he's admiring more. Either way, I know I've caught his attention.

"Welcome, everyone," he greets the class after shaking his head slightly like he's ridding a thought from his mind. "Okay, let's talk about evidence. What is it? How important is it? And what are the rules of evidence?"

"Evidence is everything. Without it, you don't have a case," Alex yells out.

"True. But are there rules to it?" he questions.

"Of course there are. There are rules to everything," Ashley retorts.

"Yes," he drawls out, "But aren't rules made to be broken?" He winks at me, and I laugh.

"Some, but not all," Charlie bites out, making me turn to look at him.

"Elaborate then," Cole urges on.

"Some rules are there for a reason. To protect people. To make sure things are fair."

"Yes, but when it comes to evidence, what is considered fair?"

"Evidence is evidence. That's the point. The word itself means it's a fact, so if it's there then it has to be fair because it's the truth."

"True, but what if it was collected illegally?" Cole argues back.

"It's still a fact," Ashley states.

"Yes, but is it admissible in court?"

"It depends on the means of how it was obtained," I yell out.

Cole eyes me suspiciously. "Give me an example of what you mean."

"Well"—I change the position of my legs, purposely uncrossing them and changing sides, so my shoes stand out—"for example, if a cop breaks into your house without a warrant and finds the gun you used to kill someone, that's protected under the Fourth Amendment and therefore thrown out in court. But"—I uncross my legs again, leaning in, putting my arms on the table, pushing my breasts up to him and going in for the kill—"say in the movie *Top Gun*"—I watch him narrow his eyes and swallow hard. I can tell his wheels are turning—"when *Maverick*," I slowly say his name, "turns the plane upside down and Goose takes a picture of them flipping off the enemy, it might have been illegal to turn the plane upside down like that, but if they had to use the picture in court to prove something, as evidence, it would be allowed since the way they obtained the photo was not illegal under the Fourth Amendment."

I've got him. I watch as realization finally hits, and he knows who I am. Darkness fills his eyes as his tongue sticks out to lick his suddenly dry lips.

"That'd be something you would do. Huh? Would you be *Maverick* or *Goose* in that situation?" I say, emphasizing Maverick to seal the deal and see his reaction.

He doesn't respond. Just stares at me, and it's not until Charlie moves his chair, causing a harsh noise to fill the silent room that the trance he had on me breaks. I smirk, sitting back in my chair and winking at him.

He nods his head slightly in recognition. "Good point, *Angie*. And yes, I think I would be *Maverick* in that situation."

"I knew it. And yeah, you can call me by my real name now. It's Evangeline."

I smirk, and I swear I see the bulge in his pants get a little bigger before he turns back to the board and clears his throat, trying to get on with the rest of his lecture.

A freedom I haven't felt in years runs through my soul. I told him to call me Evangeline more to prove a point that it's truly me, but I got more than I bargained for.

I got me back.

At this moment, suddenly, I feel like myself for the first time in years. And even more exciting, I'm happy about it.

"Ang—I mean, Evangeline," Cole calls out as I pack my bags at the end of class. "Do you have a moment?"

I look up, smiling at him. The class was difficult to get through tonight; I'm not going to lie. Knowing Cole is Maverick and that he knew it was me proved to take my attention elsewhere, and I couldn't focus for shit. Our eyes caught each other's every five seconds it felt like, and after having to readjust himself multiple times, he finally sat down for the remainder of the lecture.

I take my time packing my bag, waiting for more of the class to pour out. I notice Charlie takes longer than the others and finally leaves with a slight huff as he storms out.

I sit back in my seat once the room is empty, crossing my hands over my desk. "You wanted to talk to me, *teacher*?"

He smirks, and it's honestly the sexiest thing I've ever seen. It's written all over his face with that simple tilt to his lips. He's imagining being inside me, taking control over my body and me falling to his every demand Saturday night.

We sit in silence, staring at each other, willing the other person to say something. Our game is on, and I feel my panties moisten instantly as my heart rate picks up speed.

"So…" He taps his fingers on his desk. "Evangeline, huh? What a beautiful name."

"Thank you," I whisper, suddenly more affected by his trance.

"It really is you?" He slowly stands up, walking over to where I am.

Instinctively, I clench my legs together, holding my breath without even noticing it and looking straight ahead. Once he gets to my desk, standing tall by my side, his fingers brush out, slightly touching my face. I turn to look up at him, slowly releasing the breath I was holding when my eyes reach his.

His presence overwhelms me, and the reality of the situation starts to slowly take over. It was one thing being next to him with a mask on and another thing watching him from afar while he taught the class. But now, here, with no one around, just the two of us. It's different. I know what this man can do to me. I know what he feels like when he pushes inside me, when he licks me just the right way.

I look away, needing a second to regroup.

His fingers slightly touch me under my chin, turning me back to him, sending chills throughout my entire body. Instantly, I'm stuck in his trance again, and I'm motionless as I watch him slowly move his lips to mine.

I'm done for. The feeling of him overwhelms all of my senses except one. The only one I don't want to feel. The one I've avoided for too long, and I don't want to feel it ever again.

"Carter," I say the second his lips leave mine.

My arms grab hold of his neck as my legs wrap around his waist. His movements have slowed, and the way he's slowly thrusting inside me while kissing my neck is about to drive me somewhere I've never been. I've had orgasms while he's played with my clit or gone down on me, but this is a different feeling altogether. It's so deep, so raw, and so unbelievably amazing.

"Carter, God, what are you doing to me?" I pant out.

"I feel you, Evangeline, let go. I'm here. I'll catch you, I promise. I always will."

His lips meet mine again as his hands grip my own, and I scream instantly, exploding from the inside, and he stills, pressing hard against me, feeling every ounce of relief my body gives as I clench and then melt into him.

It's so perfect, so right. I had no idea sex could be like that, and now that I know, I want it with him, like this, for the rest of my life.

No. Forget about it. That feeling can lead to nothing but heartache, and I need to leave. Now.

I push him off me. "I'm sorry," I say as I reach down for my bag and run out of his classroom, not sure if I'll ever return.

Chapter 15

EVANGELINE

I missed class on Wednesday; I couldn't bring myself to face him. At least not in that way. Now it's Thursday, and I'm itching to go to the club. That's all I want from him. All I need.

When he kissed me in class things got too real, too intimate. Tonight will be a test, another game, and I'm hoping I come out ahead.

Nerves wreck my stomach as I pull the mask down over my head. The club opens at nine, and it's past ten now. I wanted to go late to see if he'd wait for me or if he'd go to someone else.

Scanning the room, I see both him and Secret standing next to each other. Funny, this whole week I haven't thought about this mystery guy, yet here he is again. I never even considered if Cole would tell him who I am.

Then it hits me; I have no idea if *they* even know who each other are.

I'm a little surprised to see them both standing there, engaging in their own conversation, seemingly oblivious to the multiple scenes unfolding around them. I want to believe they're waiting for me.

I tear my eyes away, walking toward a scene and sitting on the couch in front of it to watch. Not long after I sit down, a man I've never seen before approaches me.

"Are you looking for some fun tonight?" he says.

"No, she's not," I hear a deep voice radiate through the room, and I know it's Secret, still disguising his voice.

I turn to face him. "I'm sorry, did he ask you?" I taunt back.

A smirk fills his face as he starts to walk toward me. I see Cole behind him, keeping his distance, which helps me breathe a little better.

His large frame towers over me. He looks at the guy on my right before looking back at me. "Don't be sorry." He pauses. "But I don't believe our game is over yet."

He eyes the guy, tilting his head to the side, and he gets up without a second word, showing his respect toward Secret and leaving us alone.

"You think you can just run people away like that?" I bite out.

"You really think he could fuck you better than Maverick?" he whispers close to my ear before looking over at where he's standing close by.

Cole's quick to stand behind me, placing his hand softly on my face and brushing my blond hair to the side. I look up at him, not sure what to say.

"Evangeline," he barely gets out, like he's in pain to say it.

I'm glad he didn't say Angie, but the softness of his voice hits my stomach like a punch to the gut.

I take a deep breath, looking at Secret. "How come I don't know your name?"

He doesn't respond, just shakes his head.

"And how come you barely talk and when you do you disguise your voice?"

"Because it excites you," he says in an even deeper voice.

Cole's hands run down my shoulders, around to the front and grip my breasts, stroking them softly.

"Just like that excites you. Doesn't it?" Secret asks.

My head drops back. He's right. I do like it.

"You like to be fucked. You like for people to see you." He leans in, whispering softly in my ear, "And I like watching you."

He starts to lean away, but I stop him, grabbing the back of his head and bringing his lips to mine. He's frozen at first, his lips locked in place as his body goes rigid. I loosen my grip, not sure how to take his body language, but I don't let him go fully. Instead, I lick his closed lips with mine, slowly and seductively, hoping he'll soften.

A deep growl comes from his mouth as he opens up, letting me in and sweeping his tongue with mine. His large hands wrap around my body, pulling me into him, and in seconds, I'm underneath him on the couch. His kisses turn feverish, uncontrollable, but fucking amazing.

Every touch, every nibble, every lick takes me higher and higher, and I quickly find myself wrapping my legs around him, bringing him closer to me and thrusting my body against his.

His kisses are taking me completely away. For a second, I forget where we are, who I am, or that anyone else is around. All of my senses are on high alert, and all pointed directly to having him fuck me right here and now.

When I feel Cole brush my hair back, everything comes back in one quick second. "I hate to be the bearer of bad news, but club rules say you can't fuck on the couches," he says nonchalantly, but only looking at Secret, who quickly gets off me and sits next to me.

I wish I could see Cole's eyes. I'm not sure if he's telling the truth or if he wanted us to stop for his own selfish reasons. When I look at Secret, he's like a statue, looking straight-forward but the twitch in his jaw gives him away. He's pissed.

Did Cole tell him? Did he stake his claim on me? Why else would he be mad?

I reach out, placing my finger on his lightly covered jaw, trying to ease the tension through just my touch.

He shakes his head slightly and gets up to walk away.

I glare at Cole then back at Secret as he walks out of the club.

I stand up to leave, but Cole stops me.

"I'm not yours," I demand. "This is all supposed to be for fun."

"Shhh," he whispers. "I didn't tell him, I swear."

"Then what was that?"

"He has other issues." He waves them away like they don't matter.

"So you know him outside of the club?"

"You know I'm not going to answer that." He tilts his head to the side, making sure I don't ask any more questions.

"Don't act like a jealous boyfriend trying to break up our kiss."

"Whoa, where the hell did that come from? First, I'm not a jealous boyfriend; I was just following the rules. Second, don't blame him leaving on me. We can still have a good time tonight."

I shake my head, not sure what I believe. All I know is I feel like I just had the best kiss of my life, and he stopped it. Confusion clouds my brain, so instead of trying to figure out what's really going on, I turn to walk out of the club, and he doesn't stop me.

CARTER

I'm so fucked. Every part of me. But God, that kiss. I was shocked she tried, but once she got my doors to open the flood came rushing through the gates.

For the first time in years, I saw the sunshine through a dark window that's been boarded shut. If Cole hadn't stopped us, I would have fucked her right there.

My hand grips the shot glass in front of me, and I tilt my head back, feeling the burn rush past my throat and down my body.

"Want to tell me what all of that was about?" I hear Cole's voice beside me as he pulls up a chair. I should have known he'd know where I'd go.

"Why aren't you at the club?" I ask.

"I'm here to ask you the same thing. Is there something I should know?"

I turn to him. Not sure what to say. I'm not ready to spill everything. Not ready to admit out loud that this is her, the girl who ripped out my heart and left me with nothing.

"She's gone," I hear Kaitlyn say over the phone.

"What do you mean she's gone?"

"Carter, no one has heard from her in over a week. She didn't even come to her parents' funeral," she says in disbelief.

I've been blowing her phone up and calling everyone she knows. It's been torture being so far away, but I had midterms and couldn't go back home. My teachers were apologetic, but college is ruthless, and they wouldn't give me a retest since it wasn't an actual family member.

"Her aunt is here from Texas taking care of all of their affairs, and even she doesn't know where she is. Evangeline's name was on their bank accounts, so she wiped them out the day after the accident, and no one has heard from her since."

"What the hell? She can't be by herself. Where would she have gone?" I'm beyond stressed. I'm worried like crazy that she's alone, and I need to find her.

"Carter? There's something I think you need to know," she timidly says.

"What? Tell me," I demand.

"She's going to kill me for telling you this, but someone else needs to know."

"What?" I yell out.

"She called me that night, the night her parents died. She was crying and said she stormed out of her house because she got in a fight with them."

"What about?"

"I can't help but think that she feels their death was her fault. I'm sure they were looking for her when they got into the accident. We had just had our first freeze of the year, and the roads were really slick. Add in the drunk driver, and they never stood a chance."

"Kaitlyn, what did they fight about?" I interrupt her story, trying to get to the point.

"Carter"—she takes a deep breath—"Evangeline is four months pregnant."

My heart stops. I can't even breathe, and I start to feel the phone slip through my fingers and fall to the floor.

I slam my hand down on the counter, shaking my head. I look at the bartender, pointing for another shot.

"Why are you here?" I ask, gritting my teeth together.

He lets out a short laugh. "I'm here to ask you the same thing. She left after you did. This girl." He shakes his head, but a grin forms on his face.

"What?" I glare in his direction.

His smile fades, and he stares for a second. I get the feeling he wants to tell me something, but he doesn't. Instead, he gets up, slapping his hand on my back. "Never mind, bro. Not important, I guess."

I take the shot back, staring forward as I say, "If it's not important then why don't you leave?"

"Fuck, dude. You're pathetic, you know that. If this is over that chick, Satan, then I'm out. You need to get her out of your mind, and it will all start with that fucking tattoo. You'll never be rid of her if you have her memory staring back at you every day. Whatever. Have fun wallowing in your screwed-up head."

He gets up to leave, and I don't try to stop him. I need to be alone right now.

Chapter 16

EVANGELINE

Friday night looms its ugly head over me, and I know I have to go to school. I can't miss two nights in a row, and I don't want Cole to ruin my dreams of becoming a lawyer.

After last night, when Secret left, I started thinking more about Cole. I'm not sure why I got so freaked out beforehand, but I'm an adult. I can do this. What we have is sex, and I've always been able to keep my emotions out of it.

The club has flipped all of my normal relationship thinking upside down and honestly, I have no clue why. It shouldn't. I mean, I've had flings with a lot of people. I wouldn't say I'm a slut, but I like sex and don't do relationships. So there you go. Why I treat Cole any differently than anyone else I've had sex with is beyond me.

I enjoyed being with him, so there's no reason to not have more. Knowing he's my teacher could be fun, and who knows, maybe we can make the club work too.

I got all pissy when he stopped my kiss on the couch, but I spoke to Kamii, and he was right, rules dictate no sex on the couches. I guess that was my stupid head reading into things that weren't really there.

I've decided I'm not going to stress. I'm not going to get all emotional, and I'm going to have a good time like I always do.

With a renewed sense of being, I walk into the classroom with my head held high. "Hello, Professor Spence," I say as I sit in my seat.

"Angie," he pauses, surprised I'm here and even more surprised that I'm smiling.

"I told you, it's Evangeline," I say, as I take out my laptop and give him a wink when I look back up.

A sexy-as-sin smirk covers his face, and I'm glad he's catching on that I'm going to be okay with this little secret we have between the two of us.

Class goes smoothly, and before he can stop me, I pack my bags and walk out the door. When I get to my car, though, I don't leave.

He's definitely flirted with me in class, and tonight was no different, except I can tell Charlie has caught on and that he's not happy about it. He seems like a goody-two-shoes type and one who always follows the rules. If we're going to keep this up, we have to be slyer since I don't want Cole getting in trouble.

Once I watch the last student leave, I open my door and walk back in. Cole is just finishing cleaning off the board, and I close the door. The loud thud radiates through the room.

Cole jumps slightly when the sound hits him, but his tension fades the moment his eyes meet mine.

"So, Maverick." I smile as I walk down the steps of the lecture hall closer to him. "Tell me, do you ever get carnal knowledge of a female in that bar?" I ask, quoting the movie.

He lets out a small laugh before walking to his desk and leisurely pulling the seat out to sit down. His hands fold over one another as he leans back, eyeing my every move.

Once I reach his desk, I walk around to the front, pushing myself up to sit in front of him. After kicking my shoes off, I place my feet on either side of his chair, spreading my legs to reveal the garter belt I have on under my skirt.

His eyes dance up my legs, and I watch his tongue slip out, licking his lips when his eyes reach his final destination.

No words are said as his hands slide up my thighs, teasing the lace at the top of my stockings before moving up and brushing them lightly over my panties.

"I was afraid I'd lost you," he says as he pushes them to the side, running his finger up my slit.

"I didn't get my fix last night, so I took a gamble," I say, throwing his words back at him from the first day of class.

His lips tilt up in recognition. "Is that all I am, a fix?" His fingers penetrate me right as he says fix.

My head falls back, loving the feeling of his fingers inside me. When he curls them up, hitting me right on my G-spot, he growls, "Is this what you want?"

I lift my head to answer him, "God, yes."

Our eyes meet and without our masks on things feel different. I can see him now, he feels more real, and this feels dirtier, sitting on his desk, in the middle of his classroom. I look over at my desk, and instantly, I feel the excitement rush over me like I traded one kink for another.

"Ah, you like that, don't you? You like knowing you're going to fuck your teacher?"

I bite my lip, nodding my head and grinding my ass down on his desk.

"My, my, you are a dirty girl, and I like your kind of kink."

He winks, curling his hand more and pushing harder against me. His other hand reaches up, unbuttoning my blouse and pushing my bra to the side. His fingers pinch my nipple, and the sensation sends me in the other direction.

I hate that I've never liked my nipples being played with but call me crazy, I don't.

My head shakes back and forth as I grind my hips, wanting to ask him to stop but words fail me as I dig in search of my release.

Thankfully, he gets my drift and lets go, fully gripping my entire breast and kneading it softly. I groan my approval, and his lips tilt up slightly, knowing he's done well.

His fingers pull out and quickly move to my waist, sliding my panties down my legs and off completely. Giving me a devilish grin, he opens his desk drawer, sticking them inside and shutting it with a hard thump.

"I hope you didn't want those back." He winks, and I drop my head back with a laugh.

With a quick movement, his belt is undone, and he's ripping open a condom he had in his back pocket.

"Did you really just have that on you?" I tease.

"A guy can dream, right?"

I eye him suspiciously.

"I was hoping you'd walk in today, and I'd get to fuck you over my desk." He positions himself perfectly against me. "And look." He slams inside of me. "I got my wish."

My arms rush up, grabbing on for dear life to his shoulders as his thrusts speed up, beating against me. His desk starts to slide across the floor, but he doesn't stop. His movements are rushed, harsh, and I'm shocked to feel the burn deep and low starting so fast.

"We may be alone now, but someone could walk in any minute," he grunts out.

The thought of being caught rushes through my body and my burn turns into a fire, blazing out of control as I grind harder against him, so close to exactly what I came for.

I hear his heavy breathing in my ear. "Fuck Evangeline, that turned you on even more, didn't it? You want us to get caught, don't you? You want someone, say, Charlie, to walk in and see me with my cock in you."

"Oh, God," I scream out, riding out my climax that his dirty words brought on faster than I've ever felt before. He doesn't stop his stride, continuing to pound away on me as my clinching subsides, not fully enjoyed, but still amazing.

His hands grip my ass, pulling me into him as he grunts out his release and drops his head to my shoulder, biting it softly.

Our haze of pleasure is short-lived, and he pulls out, sliding off the condom and throwing it in the trash. I jump off his desk, satisfied with my choice to come back and happy knowing this was a quick fuck and nothing else.

"Thanks for that extra lesson, Professor Spence," I taunt as I start to walk away, smoothing my skirt down to where it belongs.

His hand reaches out, grabbing my ass and wrapping his other arm around my neck, bringing my back to his front.

"That. Will. Happen. Again," he forces out. "Why don't we go get a bite to eat now?"

I turn around to face him. "Nope. That's all I wanted. Thank you."

He shakes his head slightly. "Tomorrow then. Will you be at Bridge?"

"Is your friend coming back?" I ask.

"What does that matter?"

"You said you like my kind of kink." I lean in to kiss his cheek. "And my kink is him watching."

I wink and walk to the door, not turning around but knowing he's watching my every step.

Chapter 17

CARTER

"Well, don't you look like shit," Kyle states, surprising the hell out of me as I walk into his room.

"Who are you to cuss?" I throw back at him.

"Come on, I'm eleven." He rolls his eyes like that makes him old. "But don't change the subject. What's up with you?"

I ignore his question, lifting up his chart and reading any notes I missed while I was off.

"Girl problems," he calls out like he's all-knowing.

I laugh, dropping the chart down to my side. "What would you know about girl problems?"

"Believe me, I know. Sophia's going home in a few days." He looks defeated, and I know the feeling all too well.

"You can keep in touch with her." I try to cheer him up, sitting down next to him on the chair.

"Yeah, but if I don't get out of here soon, she'll move on."

"You're almost there," I say, hitting his arm slightly.

"So tell me, what girl's got you in a funk? Did you finally ask a girl out, and she turned you down?"

"What makes you think I got turned down?" I ask, surprised.

"Because if she said yes, then your face wouldn't look like that," he teases.

"Come on, I don't look that bad," I say, turning to the mirror in his room and seeing he's right. I look like shit. I keep my beard trimmed short, but it's grown much longer and is in desperate need of a trim to at least even out the growth. And my hair, it's beyond needing a haircut. I keep it cut very short normally, but now, I look like I'm trying to grow it out long, which really doesn't suit me.

Then there are my eyes; the deep, black circles under them are ones I haven't seen in years. They are the same ones Evangeline caused years ago. It's a mixture of sleep deprivation and drinking too much that displays all over my face.

I glance at my watch. He's my last patient on my rounds, and I don't have any place to be for an hour, so I decide why not. I've been needing to get things off my chest and who better to tell than an eleven-year-old boy.

I shake my head at the crazy thought but pull up a chair anyway. "So you want to know?"

"Um, yes," he demands. "I have to live my life through other people since I'm stuck in here, and I bet your life is way more interesting than mine will ever be."

I laugh out loud. "I highly doubt that. Remember that girl I told you about the other day?"

"Your first girlfriend?"

"Yeah, that's the one. Well, I found her."

"I didn't know you lost her," he jokes.

"Actually, yes, I did. Or rather, she disappeared."

"Shut up. How does someone just disappear? What did you do?"

"Why do you think I did something?" I say, trying to act offended, and he gives me a knowing tilt of his head, so I continue. "Her parents were killed in a car accident, and instead of dealing with it, she ran."

"What...?" he draws out, surprised.

"Yup. I've spent years searching for her, and guess what, she just appeared, out of nowhere."

"What did you say?"

"That's the thing. She doesn't know I found her."

"You haven't talked to her? Dude, why not? Are you chicken or something?"

I chuckle, shaking my head at the thought of the club, and that there's no way I can tell him everything. "Let's just say, it's complicated."

"Don't pull that on me. I may be a kid but don't treat me like one. Tell me."

I drop my head, shaking it slightly, and try to hide my face at the ridiculousness of this moment. "Sorry, little man. Some things I just can't say."

"Fine," he says, crossing his arms over his chest and pouting.

"I'll tell you this. I have talked to her, but she doesn't realize it's me." He looks over, a confused expression on his face. "Just go along with it, okay?"

He lets out a big huff. "Fine. Have you changed or something? How could she not know?"

I think about ten years ago to the kid I was back in Minnesota. "Yeah, I guess I have. Back then all I cared about was school and getting a scholarship so I could get out of my small town. Then she disappeared, and I lost my mind. If I wasn't studying, I was getting my frustration out at the gym. So yeah, these muscles"—I hold them up, just to play with Kyle, and he rolls his eyes at me, showing off—"I didn't have these back in high school. Or this beard." I run my fingers over my scruff, mentally noting I have to trim it tonight.

"So tell her it's you."

"Like I said, it's complicated."

His face says it all. He thinks I'm being dumb. "How complicated could it be? Do you still like her?"

I pause. Throughout these past few days, that's the one thing I didn't think about. Do I? I've gone through so many emotions the last ten years. I've missed her. I've hated her. I've loathed her. But do I like her still? I've changed so much, I can only assume she has too.

"If it's taken you this long to answer then I'm going to say you do," he blurts out.

"What makes you so wise on relationships?"

"Do you know how much television I watch?" He raises his eyebrows, nodding his head. "Look, you obviously still have something for this girl, or you wouldn't be like this right now." He holds up his hands, moving them up and down my body like he's disgusted. "And, where did you run into her again?"

I have to stop myself from cracking up at the thought. "Nope, definitely can't tell you that."

"So you know I'm an eleven-year-old boy, right? My mind can think of some pretty crazy things, and I'm going to think the worst since you won't tell me."

My head drops as my shoulders shake. His worst is nowhere near the actual truth. I guarantee that.

"Whatever," he says in frustration. "So my mom always says things happen for a reason. It ticks me off because, hello? Then why am I here? But never mind that. You say she came to you, out of nowhere. That had to have happened for a reason. So I say go for it."

I hit his arm. "You're a pretty cool little dude, you know that?"

He shrugs his shoulders. "Yeah, I know, but I'm not that little."

Chapter 18

CARTER

It's crazy how an eleven-year-old boy can put things into perspective for you. After I had finished my rounds, I went out to get a haircut and a shave. Instead of grabbing a six-pack, I stopped by the health food store and got a fresh juice, trying to rejuvenate my body and get ready for tonight.

I haven't talked to Cole, but I'm not worried if he's going to be there or not. The more I thought about it, actually, the more I almost hoped he wouldn't show up. A slight guilt runs through me, but some things just are the way they are. And she was mine first. He can move on to the next like he would anyways.

I haven't decided how tonight will go. Telling her it's me isn't something I can come out and say like it's no big deal. This should be a big deal. We have history, we had love at one point.

It may be mean, but I want her to find out the way I did. I want to see if she can tell. If I'm on her mind in any way and she can put two and two together.

When I walk into the club, Cole is leaning against the bar. I look around, noticing Evangeline isn't here yet, and when my eyes meet his, I swear I see the same look of disappointment on his face that I feel.

What does he have to be sad about? Is she not coming? Does he know this already? Did something happen after I left on Thursday?

"What's up?" I ask, offering my hand to him, and he takes it, but something is off. "What crawled up your ass?" I ask when he doesn't respond.

He shakes his shoulders, acting surprised that I noticed something's not right and stands up straighter. "Nothing. Look." He tilts his head to the front door.

There she is, walking in wearing an all-black negligee. Her outfits up till now have been slutty and barely there but this is more innocent, sweeter. And fuck me it pulls on my heart more than ever.

Cole makes his move, but I grab his arm, stopping him in his tracks.

"What? You want in finally?" he asks.

I glare at him, questioning his motive. "That's what we've always done," I say nonchalantly.

"Not with this one. You scared her off last time."

"Won't happen tonight. I got this," I say, ending our conversation and walking toward her.

I place my hand on her shoulder, lightly pulling her to me and engulfing her in my arms.

"Do I get to know your name?" she asks.

I shake my head.

"Are you not going to talk?"

I shake my head again.

"Are you going to fuck me tonight?" she teases with a slight tilt to her lips.

I don't answer either way because I'm not sure yet, so instead, I wrap my lips with hers, kissing her briefly before pulling her toward a room.

"What about Mave—" she calls out, but he cuts her off.

"I'm here," he says, wrapping her in his arms and pulling her away from me.

I let him, for now, as we walk to our space. His lips are intertwined with hers, so my hands reach up, brushing them across her hair, moving the blond locks into a ponytail and pulling back slightly, giving me room to kiss her neck and breaking their kiss.

Evangeline's arms go up around my shoulders as her head falls back more. I feel Cole move closer as he lifts her negligee, kissing her stomach and wrapping his arms around her waist. I swear I feel him pulling her away from me, so I let go of her hair and place my hands on her shoulders, keeping her right where she is.

When his tug doesn't stop, I grip her shoulders harder and swing her around, so she's facing me. She lets out a small whimper of surprise, and I lace my fingers around her neck, running them through her hair as I bring her lips to mine.

For a second, I'm brought back to my senior year and our first kiss. I wanted her so badly, and I was in shock that I was finally getting the chance. That same feeling runs through me now. I can't believe she's here, in my arms. And I still feel it. It's her. It's always been her.

I go to deepen the kiss but don't get the chance when I feel Cole literally step in between us and toss her on the bed.

"What?" she yells, surprised as I am, but he's quick to lie between her legs, sliding her panties down until they're completely off.

She looks over at me before turning her attention back to him. Something's off, and she notices it too. I've never seen Cole act like this.

His licks bring her back to reality, and instantly her hands go to his head, gripping his hair and pulling hard. She glances up at me while biting her bottom lip. I may love the taste of her, but I'll choose her kisses over everything else any day.

I rush in, reclaiming my place at her lips, and her hands leave Cole's head, wrapping them around my neck and feverishly running her tongue against mine. I've been a member of this club for almost a year now, and this is the first kiss I've had like this. I know she's new to the club, but she has to know this is not the norm. This is different.

This is us.

I move my body, ready to lie next to her but am stopped when I feel her body slide away from me abruptly. I fly back on the bed, so I don't hurt her in any way, but before I can do anything, Evangeline turns to Cole and starts yelling.

"What the fuck was that for?"

Cole tries to play innocent, knowing that was anything but. "What? Just wanted to play rough, switch things up a little."

"Don't lie to me." She pushes him away and turns to me. "Sorry, *someone* here"—she glares at Cole—"has some issues tonight."

Turning on her heel, she reaches down, grabbing her panties, and leaves the room, walking straight to the door. I'm still stunned at what just went down, but Cole is quick to chase after her. Whatever is up his ass tonight got him in trouble, and he knows it. I'll let them go. Tonight must not be the night for us.

Chapter 19

EVANGELINE

I heard Cole calling after me when I tried to leave, but I told him to back off. When the guard at the front door appeared out of nowhere, Cole was quick to do as I asked. I can't believe he was being so possessive. We aren't together. This is just sex.

I'm glad I have a few days to let everything sink in and even more thankful that I never gave him my number. With it being Sunday, I know he can't get into my school records, but if he did, I'd definitely cut him off. That would be crossing the line—big time.

I'm learning quickly that being in a secret club has its drawbacks and calling my normal friends just won't work. After a restless night, I decide to call Kamii for some advice. I know she has more on her plate than my drama, but I need help.

There are only a few rings before she answers with sleepiness in her voice. "Aw, is someone not getting much sleep?" I say into the phone. "Do you want me to call you later?"

"It's okay." She yawns. "It's nice to get a little bit of normalcy in my life. What's up? Did you go to the club last night? Preston got a call saying there was a minor incident but that it didn't escalate to anything. Did you notice something going on?"

"And that's why I'm calling," I sing out. "The minor issue was me."

"Angie, no. What happened?" Kamii blurts out, concerned.

"So how did you find out it was Preston you were playing with at the club?" I ask, beating around the bush before I spill the beans.

"It wasn't until he was in my office asking me to represent him. Why?"

"Well…guess what?"

"Crap. You know someone?"

"I didn't when I first entered, but guess who's my teacher?"

"Holy schmoly! Are you serious?"

"As a heart attack."

"How did you figure out it was him?"

"Come on, I stare at the guy for three hours every other night, listening to him talk. It wasn't that hard to put two and two together."

"So which one is your teacher? Wait, we are talking about the two guys, right?"

"Yeah, Maverick is my teacher. Secret is still, well, a secret."

"He's still playing this little game?"

"Yup, and that's what brings me to calling you," I point out. "I've come out to Maverick, Professor Spence, Cole, *fuck me*, whatever I should call him," I hear her laugh but continue anyway, "and instead of letting it ruin our time at the club, let's just say we added to our experience by living out another type of fantasy in his classroom."

"Angie!" Kamii yells out in disbelief.

I grin, moving on. "Yeah, yeah, yeah, but that's not the issue. So last night, Secret—I know that's not his club name, but it's how I refer to him—anyway, he was finally coming around last night. He was actually going to join us, but Cole kept getting in between us, like he was trying to prevent it from happening, which is bullshit. We aren't together!" I blurt out in frustration.

"Ah yes, the human factor has reared its ugly head. No matter how much we try to remain anonymous, things still happen, and feelings get in the way."

"Um, you could have warned me about this part."

She sighs. "It doesn't happen to everyone, just the lucky ones," she teases.

"Oh jeez, thanks," I deadpan.

"Wait, what was the incident then?" she asks, bringing us back to the issue.

"After he pulled me away from Secret, I got mad and left. I'd had enough and put my foot down. He tried to come after me, but when the guard appeared he backed off quickly."

"So what happens now?"

"Can't you just kick him out of the club?" I jokingly ask, having no clue what I'm going to do.

"Come on, this isn't that bad," she responds.

"I know, just sucks. I've still only been with him, and I don't want him to ruin my time there."

"You know you don't have to be with him at the club. There are rules for this kind of drama, and yes, we can kick him out if he tries to stop you."

"No." I sigh. "It's not that serious. I just don't know what to do."

"Well, even if you do figure out the club situation, you still have to deal with him being your teacher. How the hell do you always get yourself in these situations?" she teases.

"Shut up," I yell out. "I swear, I'm not always like this."

"Oh yeah, what about the guy who turned out to be your neighbor's husband?"

"Stop! I had no clue that was him. I felt like shit for weeks, and you know that."

"I know, but damn, girl. It's like bad luck follows you around. Can I call you Pig-Pen from now on?"

"Ha. Ha. Ha," I breathe out, not enjoying her making fun of me. "And besides, Pig-Pen never had the dark rain cloud you're envisioning. He was the dirty kid, remember?"

"You know what I mean," she deadpans. "I wish I could help you, but you got yourself into this mess. I told you to keep the club at the club. You'll have to talk to him. Tell him if you want to continue to play with him or not. I wish I had better advice for you, but sometimes you just have to keep your big girl panties *on* and maybe not have sex with your teacher." She giggles at her little pun.

"But do I have to, Mom?" I whine, and she laughs harder.

"Bye, Angie," she sings.

"Wait, one more thing."

"Yeah?"

"I've decided to go by my real name again."

"Your real name?" she asks, confused.

"Yeah, Evangeline," I say with pride.

Kamii doesn't know anything about my past. I've worked at the law firm longer than her and was only assigned to her desk around two years ago. I watched as she came out of her shell. And even though my shell is a different kind, I'm ready to break through mine as well.

"That's your real name? How did I not know this? And why the hell do you use your real name at the club?"

"It's a long story, but yeah, it feels good being called it again. It's been years. I walked away from who that girl was, and I feel like she's finally coming back to me."

"I'm glad to hear, Evangeline. It's a beautiful name."

"Thank you. Give that beautiful daughter of yours a kiss for me."

The time is finally here, and I can't put off walking in to my class anymore. I have to face Cole, and I hope it goes smoothly. Otherwise, I'm facing the longest class of my life.

I walk in after the lecture had already begun, and he pauses long enough to make me look up at him, seemingly unaffected by my presence.

The longer the class goes by, the easier it is to breathe, and my fear subsides. A few times I caught him looking at me, and I swear I saw the apology I hoped for written all over his face.

After class, I walked up to his desk, apologizing for being late. We played the student/teacher role, talking about what I missed last week when I didn't come to class but when that last door closed, it was like a switch was flipped and he had me in his arms before I could think straight.

"Wait," I say, pushing him back.

"No, let me say something first. I didn't mean to piss you off on Saturday," he begs.

"But you did. What the hell was that?"

"I was just playing the part." He shrugs, trying to act innocent.

"Bullshit." I push back from him. "That was the work of a jealous boyfriend, and you and I are *not* together."

He reaches for me again. "I know that."

"Do you? I'm new to this club, but I'd say that shit you pulled was not cool. I'm sure Secret didn't approve either."

"Secret?" He laughs out loud. "His name is—"

"Stop!" I hold my hand up. "You already fucked up once, please don't do it again."

"I didn't fuck up," he whispers, pulling me close with his puppy dog eyes.

"You did." I stand my ground.

"Then do you forgive me?" He tilts his head to the side.

"Can you act like an adult next time we're at the club? I'm not yours, you know? I may decide to fuck some random guy one night. That's what this club is for. You have to be okay with that."

"I am, I promise. I'll let you play with whoever you want." He pulls me in closer, so our bodies are touching. "As long as I get to fuck you too."

He leans in for a kiss, and I push him back. "We'll see about that. You'll have to prove it to me first." I lean down to pick up my bag from the floor.

The anger in me is wavering, but I'm not ready to give in just yet. He needs to know I won't stand for shit like that.

"But the club doesn't open for three more days."

"Yup. We'll see if you can be a good boy first then we can discuss us playing again, here or in the club." I turn and walk out of his classroom, feeling really good about putting my foot down.

Chapter 20

EVANGELINE

Work has been insane this week. Another firm has asked us to join them in a major lawsuit, and with Kamii still out on maternity leave, a lot more has fallen on my plate than before. She's only a phone call away, so I can ask her for guidance, but otherwise, it's perfect practice for what I hope will be my future.

"Are you joining us, Angie?" I hear Tom, one of the firm's partners, say as he peeks his head into my office.

I'm riding on cloud nine right now, so honored that not only are they allowing me to somewhat step in for Kamii, but they actually want me to sit in on the meetings and really want my opinion.

"Yup." I grab my notepad and head out to attend the biggest meeting of my career.

In a man's world, I'm not surprised that when I walk into the conference room, all I see are suits, of all colors and sizes, but when my eyes land on one, grabbing my attention in ways it shouldn't, my heart sinks.

Cole.

"Gentlemen," I say in greeting, trying not to bring any more attention to him than necessary. I almost want to look up to see if I still have that gray cloud following me like Kamii suggested. Truly, I have fucked up luck sometimes.

Everyone takes their seat, and of course, the only one left is right next to him. I pull out my chair, and his eyes greet mine, his tongue quickly licking his lips. I'm glad he hasn't brought attention to us, but my nerves are the last thing I want in this meeting.

After I pull my chair in, I feel his leg come much too close to mine, and I cough my surprise.

Mario, the head attorney on the case, gives us the rundown of what we're up against. It's a sexual harassment lawsuit against the CEO of a major corporation. The guy is a family man and swears up and down this is a money grab by the three different women accusing him.

Everything is hearsay, but as we all know, it will take strong evidence to get him off. Even though he knows the odds are against him, he's willing to drop millions to make an example as to not mess with him and draw this entire case out in court rather than just pay off his accusers. He wants it done fast, though, before public opinion sets in, so they are bringing our firm on to find a way to prove them wrong as fast and accurately as possible.

"Angie," Tom says. "We're going to need you doing a lot of research on the accusers. Talk to everyone you can. If you need to go back to their preschool teacher then do it. Dig up any dirt on these people that you can find."

Mario adds in, "This is Cole next to you. You two work together, bounce ideas off each other, compare notes and come up with a game plan." He throws a stack of papers bound together by a clip on the table. "This is what our client came up with so start here. Then talk to their friends, neighbors, ex-bosses, anyone you can. Their women are good, but we're better."

Cole grabs the stack of papers. "On it," he says before looking at me. "Looks like we have our work cut out for us. Hope you're a coffee drinker." He smiles, and yes, I feel it deep and low, and I cross my legs in response. The tiny laugh on his lips makes me want to hit him.

The meeting continues and afterward I walk to my office, thinking I got off scot-free until I hear the light wrap of knuckles hitting the door.

"Yes," I say, hoping it's someone from my firm and not him. If only I were so lucky.

His tall frame enters my office, giving me a sexy smirk as he closes the door behind him.

"How did I get so lucky?" he says, walking to my desk.

I stand up. "Stay right there," I urge. "This is my workplace. I need this job, and I can't screw up this opportunity."

"I wouldn't dare put you in any situation to get you in trouble." He holds his hands up like he's not guilty, but the look on his face says anything but.

He slowly makes his way toward me, and I've never been so glad my desk is as big as it is, keeping him at a safe distance from where I stand.

Placing his hands on the surface of my makeshift barrier, he leans in, whispering, "I will, however, enjoy every aspect of this case because I get to know you better. So, dinner, my place, say five o'clock?"

"Smooth, real smooth, but no. Let's meet here. We can have takeout delivered." I may be a freak, and I may like to fuck, but I know there's a time and place, so being here, at my work, will keep me in line. This isn't a relationship; this is work.

"You don't have to worry. I'll be a good boy. I promise." He crosses his heart and winks before turning to leave.

"See you tonight, Evangeline."

At five o'clock, there's a knock on my office door, and I know the time has come. Instead of telling him to come in, I stand up, opening the door myself, ready to escort him to the conference room. Being in my small office would be too claustrophobic. We need a large space, with windows on either side if we're going to work together.

I take a seat on one side of the table and am happy when I see him sit on the other side.

"See, I can be a good boy," he teases.

I grin before letting out a sigh of relief. This might work.

We open the files, laying everything out on the table, but before we start, Cole grabs his phone. "So what are we ordering in?"

"There's a great Chinese place down the street that delivers," I respond.

After looking up the number, he places an order for way too much food, and we open the files, getting started on a game plan.

This is a completely different side of Cole I'm seeing. I've seen the teacher, I've seen the sex god, shoot, I know him personally. But this, this is different. This is the professional Cole, and I like that I get to see every aspect of him.

Our food arrives shortly after we get started. Cole gets up to greet the delivery guy downstairs and brings the bags up to our floor.

"How much do I owe you?" I ask, reaching for my purse.

"Evangeline, really? I can buy you dinner without it meaning anything."

"Well, thank you," I say, looking back at my files.

"Come on. We can eat first. I won't bite. I promise," he says, handing me a plate.

I give in. He's right. We can take a break to eat. It's going to be a late night as it is.

"So, Evangeline, tell me about your name. Why did you go by Angie when Evangeline is such a beautiful name?"

"Nope. Not going there." I eye him.

He smirks. "Okay, then let's start with something else. Where are you from?"

"Where are you from?" I ask back.

Knowing I'm not going to go there, he starts talking. "I grew up not far from here actually. Can you believe I was kind of a scrawny nerd in high school?"

He laughs, and I can't help but join in with him. It takes a big man to make fun of himself.

"Back then glasses weren't as sexy as they are now." He plays with his glasses, pushing up his eyebrows at the same time. "Don't try to hide it. You liked seeing them in class the first time."

I smile a knowing smile but don't give him the satisfaction of actually saying it, but yes, his glasses were a turn on in a weird way. They aren't your normal reading glasses. They're black, slim-framed, and very retro.

"That's why I wear them, you know. It makes the girls horny." He grins at his own joke.

"Then why don't you wear them at the club?"

"Glasses and masks don't mix. Thank God for contacts." He winks.

"So you were the nerd, huh? Is that why you're a member? Making up for your lonely high school days?" I joke.

"Nah, not really. I like the kink of being there, having someone watch me, and of course, the no strings attached thing is a plus."

"Until you met me."

"Yup, you had to come screw everything up." He smirks at me before he takes a bite of his General Tso's Chicken.

"Am I the first person's identity you figured out from the club?"

"Yes and no. I knew." He pauses, correcting himself before he says his full name. "Secret."

My lips tilt up in a silent thank you for not telling me his name. "What's his story?"

"Ha!" he belts out. "You don't want to know his name, but you want to know his story? Come on, you know I can't go there."

I bite the inside of my lip. He's right. There's something about him that I'm dying to know. He's mysterious, and it excites me in a way I never imagined.

"Is he always like this?"

He shakes his head. "Nah, he's actually never been like this, but I think he saw you liked it, so he's going with it. The first day we met you he was in a mood. That's what started it all."

"So it's not me?"

"Why would it be you?"

I shrug, playing with my food, my stupid female insecurities creeping their way up.

"Besides, that's how I've gotten to have you all to myself."

I role my eyes in his direction, and he chuckles softly. "New subject," I demand. "Besides being at an anonymous club, what else do you do for fun?"

"Music. Anything music related; concerts, record stores, searching YouTube for new bands."

"Okay, what's your poison? What kind of music do you listen to?"

"I like a bit of everything, but my favorite is new age rock. The bands that are a little hard, a little old school rock, and play a mean guitar."

"Do you play?"

"Nope, I wish. I couldn't hold a tune if I tried, but my air guitar is on point."

I have to cover my mouth to stop the food from coming out when I laugh out loud.

"What about you? Are you a music buff?" he asks.

I hold up my finger, grabbing my napkin to cover my mouth as I finish my bite. "I'm the same," I speak out. "Actually, I just saw Skillet a few weeks ago."

"Shut up. At the Filmore? I was there! I worked my way to the front, right below the girl guitarist."

"Nuh-uh, I was on the other side in front of the guy."

"They kicked ass," he states, sitting back in his chair.

"Right? I was so impressed when the drummer sang out during *Awake and Alive*. That's talent."

"I thought the same thing. I couldn't believe her voice could belt out that clear while banging away on the drums. I always thought it was the other girl singing those parts."

"Me too," I jump up, excited he thought the same thing. "She sang too, though."

"Did you know they're husband and wife? That singer and the lead guy."

"Really? I wondered who was hooking up with who."

"I'm going to see Shinedown on Thursday. You should go with me."

"I already have tickets."

He nods his head. "Nice, then I'll see you there."

"Maybe even before." I'm not sure what came over me, but I like this—just sitting with him, discussing music and hanging out. It's nice.

He grins then picks up the folder we were going over earlier, getting right back to business as we continue our dinner, discussing the case and working into the late night.

Chapter 21

EVANGELINE

Yesterday was fun. I genuinely enjoyed working with Cole, and I was impressed when at the end of the night, he didn't try anything. He insisted on walking me to my car, and when we got there, he kissed me on the cheek, whispering his goodbye in my ear and that he'd pick me up in the morning.

We made a list of everyone we should talk to, and today we're heading out to track everyone down together. I should be nervous about it, but oddly enough, I'm not. Last night was comfortable, and I'm actually looking forward to spending the day with him.

Against my better judgment, I gave him my home address, and when I hear the knock on my apartment door, butterflies swirl lightly in my stomach. When I open the door, the sexy guy I first saw in class greets me but in a completely different way.

The first day I saw him he was wearing jeans and looked like a laid-back kind of guy. Now the man before me is wearing a tailored suit, with his dark hair lightly gelled, making it look sexy yet put together.

His smile, though. Man, he's got one that can knock any girl on her ass.

"Well, hello, Evangeline," he greets me with a grin.

I'm still getting used to hearing my name again and coming from his lips makes my heart pitter-patter more than I want it to.

I might actually be falling for this guy.

I turn quickly, trying to hide the flush from my face, and grab my purse.

"So who's first?" I ask as we slide into his Audi S4.

"I mapped out our trip." He hands me a map with way too much detail on it.

"You're kidding, right? You really are a nerd," I tease.

"Ha. Ha," he deadpans. "I'm prepared. I don't miss anything or waste any time." He smirks before pulling away from the curb as we head to the first spot on the printed map and discuss our game plan.

So far the day is a bust when it comes to the case, but for everything else, it's been the best I've had in a while. Cole's had me laughing harder than I've done in years and has made me blush more times than I can count.

Now we're pulled over on 17th Street at a taco truck. "Are you sure this is safe?" I ask, staying in my seat.

He walks around, opening my door. "Come on. It's the best taco truck you'll ever have."

His hand is outstretched, offering to help me out of his low car, and I grab it. Once I'm up, though, he doesn't let go, and I allow him to keep his hold on me.

It's been a long time since I've hung out with a guy like this. Even though we're working, we've spent a lot of time in the car together today and have talked for most of it. He's told me about his family and his little sister who's just about to graduate college.

The look on his face almost made me spit out the water I was drinking when I asked how he'd feel if she joined a club like Bridge. I told him he had some massive double standards, and his only comeback was that he didn't care, and there was no way in hell.

As we approach the truck, I look up at the menu, asking, "What's *lengua*?" Trying my hardest to pronounce it correctly.

He lets out a loud laugh. "It's tongue."

I quickly turn to walk back to the car, and he laughs even harder, stopping me in my tracks. "Come on. I'll order for you." I eye him suspiciously, so he continues, "I promise, is carne asada okay? It's grilled steak."

I hit his stomach. "I know what that is. And fine. Order for me. But I'm putting my stomach in your hands."

He leans in, kissing my cheek. "I'll take whatever part of you I can get."

After ordering we walk over to some picnic tables and sit to wait for our food.

"You've really never heard of lengua? Where are you from?"

The thought of lengua makes me want to gag in my mouth again, and I have to shake off the notion. "I'm from Minnesota, from about the smallest town you can think of. And no, there's no tongue eating happening there."

"Funny, that's where—" He stops mid-sentence, shaking his head and changing his mind on the thought. Right then our order is called, and he gets up to grab the food and brings back the best smelling containers to our table.

There are two small tacos on each plate containing two corn tortillas, each topped with little chunks of what I hope to God are carne asada, along with onions, cilantro, and a lime next to each one. They look so simple yet smell amazing.

He holds up his first one and tips it up to me, saying, "Cheers," before taking a bite.

Going in for it, I take a bite and savor the tastes bursting in my mouth. I've had tacos but not like this.

"Good, huh?" he asks through a mouth full of food.

I nod my head while reaching for a napkin to cover my mouth. "Yes. Back home there aren't a ton of Mexican restaurants. Seriously, Taco Bell was about as authentic as things got and that wasn't even in my town. We had to drive a few towns over."

"I couldn't survive there. I live on Mexican food."

Thinking of Cole back in my small town makes me laugh. He's right. He couldn't survive there. He's too uptown for my hick town.

"Okay, I've got to learn where you're from. Tell me something else," he asks.

"Not much to know, really. I moved here about ten years ago, haven't ever looked back, and after working at a law firm for the past five years, I'm interested in moving up, so that's why I'm in your class."

"You weren't interested in law growing up?"

I laugh. "No, far from. I might have broken the law a few times, but never thought about fighting for it."

"Broken the law, huh? Do tell."

I shake my head, looking down, laughing but ashamed as well. "I told you, I grew up in a really small town. Well, there were only two police officers on shift at a time, so it was easy to see where they were and more importantly, where they weren't. My friend and I would trip an alarm at the local grocery store after it closed and then go do whatever the hell we wanted anywhere else in town."

"Was this friend a boyfriend or girlfriend?" he asks, and I pause, taking a deep breath.

"Hurry, go, go, go," I scream, jumping in Carter's car as he speeds away.

I can tell by the white of his knuckles he's scared shitless, but I love the rush. We get a few miles up the road before we hear the sirens and then watch the two cop cars fly by in the opposite direction.

I watch as he visibly lets out a breath and sits back more calmly in his seat. "So what now?" He turns, asking me what else I had planned for the night.

"It's you and me, baby, we can do whatever you want. We have at least an hour until they clear the alarm and get the whole thing situated," I respond.

"Water tower?" He looks at me for approval.

"Perfect!"

There's a huge tower people can climb on the outskirts. Town officials are always afraid someone's going to fall if they climb it, so it's a hotspot for the cops to patrol. I've wanted to climb it but never got the opportunity.

We park and both jump out of the car, knowing we have a time limit to our escapade.

Once we're on top, both of us lie down on our backs, close to each other, and stare up at the stars. Minnesota has an amazing view anyway, but up that much higher in the sky, without any lights surrounding you, it's truly a sight to be seen.

Carter's hand intertwines in mine, and he looks over, whispering, "I love you, Evangeline."

Before I can say anything back, his lips are on mine, and my legs wrap around his waist. I may not get the opportunity to say it back, but I can definitely show him.

I shake my head. "That's not important. Not anymore at least."

"Then definitely a boyfriend," he states with a slight chuckle, and I wish I could laugh back but not about him. Carter is never a laughing matter.

Chapter 22

EVANGELINE

Cole and I have spent every day together working on this case and then class on Wednesday night too. Now it's Thursday, and I'm not finding it a coincidence that we both have tickets to see Shinedown. Our paths seem to be aligning more than I normally like, but in this case, it's hard to fight fate.

I was going with a group of friends, but when Cole offered to take me to dinner first, it was hard to turn down. He's been the perfect gentleman this entire time. He's only kissed me a few times, but they were simple and sweet kisses goodbye. He hasn't tried to sleep with me or get me to stay at his apartment.

He says he really wants to get to know me, and I'll admit, I'm starting to fall for him, but I'm not sure I want to. I don't do relationships, and I need to make sure he knows that.

After work, we go our separate ways to get ready for the concert, but he's supposed to pick me up at seven. And right on time, my doorbell rings like a chime to start a boxing match. I take a deep breath and walk to the door, ready to set the record straight.

And then I see him. *Fuck me.* Those stupid glasses are sexy, and he's wearing those jeans again, but now his hair is styled messy, and the cheesy grin on his face is too much.

"You ready?" he asks.

I turn to grab my purse and walk out without saying anything.

"Nice ass," he says while appraising my outfit.

I went with my leggings with earphones on them and an oversized shirt that barely covers my backside, showing off the very bottom.

He leans in, pushing me against the wall and grabbing me, lifting me up in the air where I instantly wrap my legs around him. For a second, I'm lost in his touch, then his kiss, and before I can push him away, he puts me down.

"Just wanted to make sure you still tasted the same." He wipes his mouth and grabs my hand. "Yup. Still pretty fucking amazing. Now let's go."

I trip over myself as I close the door and follow after him like a lost puppy. His kiss caught me by surprise, and now I'm kicking myself that I fell into it without any hesitation.

Dinner was as casual as our days have been, and thankfully, he hasn't tried anything that would make this feel like more of a date than it is. My mind is playing tricks on me, and my not-so-smart side is totally okay acting like nothing's happening between us.

If I ignore it, it will go away, right?

The concert is at the Warfield, and both of our tickets are general admission, so we don't have to worry about not sitting with each other. My friends text me to say they're already there, and I can't believe I didn't think about the fact they might meet Cole. Concern over how I should introduce him starts to turn in my stomach. Do I say he's my friend, my teacher, my co-worker, the guy I met at a sex club?

Even I laugh at the crazy way our lives have intertwined so drastically. *Damn you, fate.*

Once we enter the venue, I don't make an effort to connect with them, and instead, Cole grabs us some drinks, and we claim our spot toward the front of the stage.

The group of friends I attend concerts with is always fun, but they never like to get up close. Fear of the moshpits keep them near the back, so it's nothing new for me to be upfront and them in the back. I look over as the opening band begins, and the excitement of the music washes over Cole's face. Music is my happy place and seeing him with the same vibe makes my heart sing.

Damn you, fate.

He looks at me before throwing his hands up in the air and dancing to the beat.

We spend the night, singing at the top of our lungs, dancing and bouncing around like we don't have a care in the world.

It's prefect.

Afterward, our voices are rough and our bodies sweaty as we make our way to his car. When we arrive at my place, he doesn't ask but instead simply parks his car and opens his door like he's home for the night and we've done this a thousand times before.

When we get to my front door, I turn to him. "What? You think you can just invite yourself in?" I tease but am serious as well.

"I wouldn't dream of it." He holds up his hands in defense.

I let out a deep sigh, not sure what to do with this.

"Hey, don't. I get it," he says. "Just because I've already gotten to fuck you doesn't mean I expect it now. We're doing things backward, and I'm okay with that. I got to fuck you when it was just sex, and now, I want to earn the chance to sleep with you when it's more than that."

"But what about the club on Saturday?"

He lets out a laugh. "Oh, that's still just fucking and believe me, I'm going to make up for this past week of being near you and not being able to have you. This." He pauses and looks around. "This is different."

"Thank you, Cole." I lean up to kiss his cheek.

He turns to walk away, but when he reaches my sidewalk, he turns back to me. "I'll earn it, too. I promise you that." He winks, and I laugh in response, watching him turn back around and hop in his car.

Chapter 23

CARTER

I knew Cole was going to miss Thursday night due to a concert he was going to. I was supposed to go with him, but at the last minute, he sent me a text saying he was bringing a date, this student he keeps mentioning. I tried to warn him again, but he swore this one wasn't going to be an issue.

His ditching me for a date isn't something new for him, and I almost expected it, was excited about it even.

This meant I was going to be alone at the club, and it might finally be my chance to reveal who I am to Evangeline. But to my dismay, she wasn't there either. After waiting until midnight, I finally threw in the towel and headed home. A few other members tried to pique my interest, but I was there for only one reason and one girl.

I called Cole Friday and even this morning to see if he wanted to play a game of basketball, but he hasn't returned my calls, just a text saying he's swamped with work, but he'd be here tonight.

I only hope she is too, and we haven't scared her off.

Cole is first to arrive, and Evangeline not far after, which rubs me the wrong way at first, but then I blow it off. *There's no way they came together.*

Tonight the club is a little bit of anything goes, so I have an idea, and I hope she's down with it.

Happiness washes over me when she walks right past Cole like she didn't even notice him standing there watching a scene and comes straight up to me.

"Hi," I grunt out in my deep voice, still trying to hide who I am. My hand reaches out to her bare waist, pulling her into me. "I have a new game I wanted to play. You down?" I say, whispering into her neck as I kiss it softly.

"I finally get the two of you, at once?" she asks, her hands roaming down my front and gripping my semi-hard cock.

What I have planned will take the two of us, but a bit of disappointment creeps up my spine. I guess deep down I wanted her to only want me.

"That's my plan. Where's Maverick?" I whisper again, not moving away from her neck and enjoying the last bit of time alone I have with her.

She pulls away slightly, looking for Cole, who's already standing to my right. *Dammit.*

I look at Cole, trying to change my sudden mood and make sure he's on board with my plan. I hold up the rope I had in my back pocket and watch as Cole's face lights up. We've talked about doing something like this but never have.

"Follow my lead?" I ask, though I'm not expecting him to say no. I'm just making sure he knows I'm in charge tonight.

He nods, stepping to the side and allowing me to pull Evangeline with me. She stops briefly, leaning up to kiss Cole, and the act surprises me. Then I remember last week when she stormed out of here. Maybe that was just her way of saying what happened was forgiven.

Tonight I want to play with Evangeline, both for my pleasure and for hers. I want to torture her, sexually. See how far I can push her to the edge before she breaks. And then, I want to see if she can tell it's me who catches her.

I walk her to a chair I have waiting in front of a scene involving five people. Every person has something going on, and it's hard to see where some bodies start and others stop.

I remove her bra, and after wrapping one rope around her wrists and tying them behind her back, I lean down in front of her, kissing my way down her belly. I slide off her panties and lick her quickly, just enough to tease her and get her wet, both on the inside and out.

"Sit down," I whisper.

She obliges, and I turn her knees out, one to each side, so she's open and on display for me. Taking the rope, I wrap it around her ankles and secure them to the edges of the chair, so she has to keep them open.

Then I walk away, grabbing Cole to follow me and leaving her there, naked and wide-open on display.

EVANGELINE

What the fuck? I look around and watch Cole walk away with Secret, leaving me here without a word. I asked him to let me play, but I didn't know I'd be getting tied up. He wasn't the one who did it, though…Secret did. Cole watched in amusement, and I'm dying to know if he was internally laughing at me because he was giving me what I wished for or if he's in on this.

A moan of pleasure sings out and grabs my attention, pulling me into the scene in front of me.

I watch as one girl is lying on her back, a guy up on his knees fucking her while a girl leans over and rubs her clit. Suddenly, I understand why Secret tied my legs the way he did.

A throb works its way through my core, and I've never noticed how much relief I get from closing my legs tightly until I don't have the ability to do so.

I turn to the other two people in the scene, but my ache gets worse when I catch a glimpse of her face and the extreme pleasure ripping through her as the guy slides in and out at a leisurely pace. The way her hands fly down on the bed, grasping for any bit of control she has left, lights my insides on fire.

The time slowly ticks away and a need growing low inside me is driving me to the brink. I squirm in my chair, looking for any type of relief but nothing works. My pussy is aching, and all I can do is stare at the cause of my plight.

I turn my head to the right and then the left, but all I see are other scenes unfolding, and thoughts of being those women makes my body tingle in anticipation.

My lips part and my head starts to bob ever so slightly with the motion of him sliding in and out of her. I'm absolutely mesmerized by my view, and I don't notice Cole behind me until I feel his hand grip my breast and a quick warm breeze blow across my open legs.

The two sensations together make my body boil, feeling like I'm going to explode. The idea that I'm finally going to get my night with both men makes me curl my toes in anticipation as I drop my head back and give my body freely to both of them.

My eyes were closed but before I can open them, my mask is removed, and a soft blindfold is tied quickly in its place. I jump at the thought of people seeing me, but Cole leans down, whispering in my ear, "It's okay. It covers the same amount as the mask. Do you trust us?"

I bite my lip and nod my head. A warm hand caresses my pussy, running his finger through my folds for a brief moment before my legs are released from their hold.

Cole lifts me from behind, and I'm walked to another part of the club. In my head, I envision the same place we've been, but honestly, I don't know, and the thought makes me tingle in ways I've never felt.

I have no clue who's watching, where they're taking me, or what's going to happen, and I swear, I've never been so turned on in my life.

I'm sat in what feels like the same chair as before, and they reposition my hands above my head, tying them to the chair again so I can't move.

To my surprise, my legs are brought up high, and I can feel a rope being tied around my mid-thigh, to my ankle and to what feels like the back of my chair as I can feel the ropes against my shoulders.

My ass slides forward slightly into a more comfortable position, and I rest my head on the edge of the chair as I listen for clues of who's who and where they are. When we walked over here I could tell, but now, they've both moved around and are being eerily quiet, so I have no clue.

The feeling of two fingers sliding up my slit takes me by surprise.

"So wet for me," Secret grunts out in his sexy Batman voice.

Another hand joins his caress, and I can't tell if it's Cole or Secret. When yet another hand wraps around my breast, just the way I like it, warmness overtakes my entire body, and I know I'm in for one hell of a ride.

Having so many hands on me at once and not having a clue who's who or where they are is intense. Take away my sight, and every touch feels ten times more sensitive, more intriguing, more mind-blowing.

They both remove their hands, and I'm left there, on display, for a minute, the anticipation killing me.

I don't feel anyone near me until the warmth of a tongue moves up my slits and wraps around my clit. Within a few seconds, I'm panting, trying to move my body in any way I can to find any kind of relief from what I've had pent up. When two fingers push inside me, curling up to the exact right spot, I scream out the most intense orgasm I've ever felt.

"Do you feel better now?" Secret whispers in my ear.

I bite my lip, nodding, still not able to actually speak.

"I'm glad that spot of yours hasn't changed," he says quickly before walking away again.

His comment has me reeling, but when I hear the tearing of a condom wrapper, all of my attention is focused on where they are and more importantly, who I'm going to get.

With my legs still tied up, a tip teases my entrance, and I shudder when he pushes in ever so slightly before pulling back out. He's playing with me, and he's fucking good at it.

"Do I get to know who's doing me tonight?" I ask.

In unison, they answer, "Both of us," with Cole in his normal voice and Secret in his grunting tone.

This teasing game is building an ache so low, so deep inside me that I want to scream and just when I think I can't take it anymore, a finger is placed lightly on my chin, turning me to the side, and when the tip of a cock touches my lips, I open up wide, welcoming him in.

As I do, I'm finally given the other man's cock fully, and he picks up his pace, sliding in and out while I suck on the other's length.

So many sensations run through me while being tied up. Taking what they're giving me and having no control over the situation brings me to the breaking point again.

The man fucking me leans over, so he's closer to my face.

"She's close, I can feel it," I hear Secret grunt.

Cole agrees, "Hell yeah, I can feel it."

They're both so close that I can't tell who's in front of me and who's directly to the side of me. Not knowing who's about to tip me over the edge is the exact push I need to send me flying again.

My mouth opens wide from around the other guy's cock as I scream and he pulls out completely, leaning down to kiss my lips.

Secret.

Now I know Cole is the one inside me still, pumping away with his own release.

I'm lost in Secret's kiss and almost forget that my legs are tied up, and Cole is still inside of me. The way his lips touch mine ignite something deep inside that's been dormant for way too long.

He starts to pull away, and I let out a whine, not wanting his lips to leave mine.

I hear his small laugh and he leans in, whispering, "It's real, isn't it?" before bringing his lips to mine again, giving me what I want. Wrapping his fingers through my hair, he kisses me like we're the only two people in the world. And for these few minutes, we are.

Chapter 24

EVANGELINE

I stayed up all night thinking both about my kiss with Secret and Cole's behavior. So many feelings are running through me; feelings I've stayed away from for years now. The thoughts have me staying in all day and hiding from the world.

Curled up on my couch in my sweats with my hair in a ponytail, I'm shocked when there's a knock on my door.

Looking through the peephole, I see Kamii, and happiness fills my body. I gladly open the door, but my smile fades when I see the infant carrier sitting on the floor in front of my place.

The sight stings my chest. I've been doing so well dealing with the birth of Becca, but with my mind going crazy from both Secret and Cole, too many memories are coming on too strong and having her spring this on me, not being able to mentally prepare, might be too much.

I try to hide my true feelings. "Hey, girl." I open the door wide, welcoming her in before taking a deep breath.

"Hi, I hope you don't mind me dropping in like this. I had to get out of the house, and I wanted to go over some stuff with you for the club, so instead of calling, I took the chance and ran." She stops to laugh. "Well, ran as fast as I could when having to get Becca ready and pack everything I need for her. Being a mom is exhausting."

I smile, but inside, all I can think is I'll never know what you mean.

We walk over to the couch, and she removes Becca from her carrier, sitting down and holding her tiny body against her chest.

"So, we have a few new members who want to come in, and one who is leaving," she states, getting right to business.

I'm still standing, not noticing that I'm staring at Becca and Kamii pauses, looking up at me. She closes the files she had opened and sits back in her chair.

"What's up, buttercup?" she asks, bringing me from my trance. "You want to talk about something?"

I plop down, defeated. "No. Yes." I shake my head and rub my eyes. "I just don't know."

"Don't know what?"

"Things. Life. Love. All of it."

"Whoa, that's a change of pace for you."

"I know. God, I'm a mess."

"You're not a mess. You're human. So tell me what's going on in that head of yours."

"It's more about what's going on in my heart," I admit.

"Really?" she asks, surprised. "What happened? Is this about your teacher?"

The entire time I've known her I've been very blasé about sex and relationships. She's heard me talk about dates I'd go on and even guys I've hooked up with at our office. All of it was for fun, nothing more. Now, here I am at a place where this kind of attitude is supposed to happen, and I'm all messed up.

"So my teacher is also a lawyer with the other firm we're working on the big case with."

"What? Really?"

"Right? So, we've been hanging out a lot working on the case together. And." I sigh. "I'm actually starting to like him."

"That's great!" She jumps up in excitement. Well, as much as she can while still holding Becca.

"Is it, though? I don't know. And then last night." I pause, not sure how to proceed.

"Yes…" she drags out, egging me on.

"It's this Secret guy. There's just something about him. Something that's bringing back memories I'm not ready to handle."

"Like what?" Becca starts to fuss, and Kamii bounces her lightly in her arms before standing up, reaching to hand her to me. "Here, can you hold her while I get her diaper ready?"

I reach out, but instantly tears fill up in my eyes as I bring her to me and memories flood my mind.

"Push, Evangeline, Push. Just a little bit more," the nurse calls out as she grips my leg high on my thigh, plastering them up to my chest.

A ripping sensation burns through me as scorching pain is being pulled from my body. "I can't. Please, I can't."

"You hear me. You can. You're almost there. You can do this."

I take a deep breath, gripping my thighs tightly as I push harder, stronger, longer than before, screaming out at the top of my lungs as the burning stops and relief flows through my body, knowing it's finally over.

Dropping back down to the bed, I take in slow, deep breaths as tears fill my eyes and overflow without any control.

Screams of happiness fill the room as the nurse rubs a washcloth across my forehead, but I turn my head, not wanting the attention.

"Hon." She rubs my arm. "Do you want to meet your baby?"

I try to curl in a ball, tears flowing with no stopping in sight as I retreat back within and shake my head.

I hear her whisper something to the other nurse before turning her attention back to me, comforting me when there's no way I'll ever recover from this. I know she's still going to try, though. Maybe she sees this kind of stuff often. Maybe she's been in my shoes. I don't know. All I do know is that was the hardest thing I've ever done, and even though my body is screaming in pain, my heart is ripped apart more than anything else.

"Whoa," Kamii says, leaning down to be eye level with me and rubbing her hand on my knee. "What are all the tears about?"

I hand Becca back to her and stand to walk to the bathroom. I need to regroup before I say anything.

Kamii leaves me alone for a few minutes before I hear a light tap on the door. "You okay in there, sweetie?" Kamii whispers through the door.

"I'll be right out," I say, fighting my tears.

All these years of hiding, pretending my past didn't happen are all coming to the front at one time. That damn picture of Carter, whatever is going on between Cole and me. Now the baby...I don't think my heart can take all these feelings squeezing their way back into my life at once.

A minute later I walk out, taking a deep breath, ready to open my soul. "I had a baby when I was eighteen," I admit as I round the corner back to the living room. Kamii turns around, her face showing so many questions, so I continue. "We were in love. At least I thought we were. He went away to college before I found out about the baby. I come from a small town, and he was so smart, even got a full scholarship to UCLA. He was going to be a doctor, and I knew if I told him he would have given it all up. I didn't want us to struggle financially or to have our baby grow up without things like we both did. I was so lost," I admit as I sit down, tears flowing freely again.

"I finally got the nerve to tell my parents, and they were so mad at me. The one thing they always stressed was not to get pregnant. They didn't want me to throw away my future by having a baby young. I left the house after yelling at them. I was already a mess about what to do, and I was angry they were so upset instead of being parents and supporting me when I needed them the most. They came after me, trying to chase me down. That's when I watched a guy run a red light, barely missing me and crashing into the side of them."

"Angie…" Kamii places Becca down on the blanket she spread out on the floor and rushes over to my side.

"That's when I ran. I left my hometown, changed my name, cut everyone off, and started over with the money they had in their bank accounts and then from selling everything off that they owned."

"What did you do with the baby?" Kamii asked.

Tears flow down my cheeks, and I cover my face as I admit, "I gave him up for adoption. I'm so ashamed. I didn't have that person I loved. I didn't even have anyone I knew by my side. I was alone. Part of me died right there on that hospital bed, and I don't know if I'll ever have it back." I cover my eyes, crying even harder.

"Oh, Angie, no, please, don't cry." Her arms wrap around me, holding me tightly as I cry for the last nine years that I've held in all of my emotions.

Once I've settled, and only a few sniffles remain, Kamii pulls away from me, moving my hair from my face and trying to look me in the eyes. "You know what?"

I look up, embarrassed by what I just admitted.

"I remember hearing once that giving your child up for adoption is actually the most motherly thing you could possibly do."

I cover my face again and start bawling. How can that be possible?

She removes my hands, making sure I'm paying attention. "You knew you couldn't provide for that child, and you wanted him to have a better life than what you could give him. You gave him up because you loved him enough to want a better life for him. That's very honorable of you."

Tears fall again as I wrap my arms around her and cry into her shoulder. "Thank you, Kamii. You have no idea what that means to me."

"Sweetie, I'm just sorry I didn't know sooner. If I had known I would have been more sensitive about bringing Becca around."

"No, please don't be sorry. It's been years. I need to move on."

"Is that what's happening with Maverick? What's his real name?"

I laugh. "It's Cole, and yes, but it was before that too. Everything seems to be coming out all at once. First, I accepted a friend request from someone back home who figured out where I was. Then she tagged me in a photo that had my ex-boyfriend in it in one of those throwback Thursday posts."

"Have you talked to him?"

Tears flow again. "No. And he doesn't know either."

"Angie..." she whispers, and I can hear the disapproval in her tone.

"I couldn't tell him. The night my parents died I called him, and not one but two girls answered his phone. He moved on and lived across the entire country, so I didn't think he needed to know. But now..." I pause, not sure what to say.

"Now you're not so sure?"

"No," I cry, covering my eyes again. "But what's the point? I'm not even sure where he is. She tagged him in the photo, and I immediately canceled my Facebook account so I wouldn't be tempted to search for him. I don't want to know what he's up to or where he is."

Her hand reaches out to hold me, reassuring me as she says, "Yeah, you do."

I can't fight the loud cries that come out as I wrap my arms around my body, holding tightly, knowing what she said is true.

"Do you want to tell him about the baby? Is it possible he already knows?"

"Honestly, I have no clue. I've cut everyone off, and until my friend found me on Facebook, I've had no contact with anyone from my past. She was the only person I told about that baby."

"So that's why you changed your name to Angie?"

I nod. "My real dad passed away when I was a baby. My mom remarried and changed my last name from Smith to Colette. So when I left, I changed my name back to Smith. When I was younger, I hated how long Evangeline was, and I wanted to change it to Angie, so I figured why not. There are tons of Angie Smiths, but I'd be shocked to find another Evangeline Colette, so I figured it was easier for me to hide."

She nods, seemingly understanding why I've done what I did. "Was the adoption open or closed?"

I look down. "Open."

"So you know where he is?"

I take a deep breath. "No. They've sent me letters, tons of them actually, but I've never opened one. Just knowing he's okay is enough for me. Seeing the envelope tells me that. So I put it in the box with all the other letters and try to go on with my life." I look up at her. "I'm just not sure if I want to anymore. Not like this anyway."

Her arms wrap around me again, holding me tightly as I cry even more on her shoulder. I have no clue what I'm going to do. I need to move on, but can I? And is Cole the right guy to even try a relationship with?

Chapter 25

CARTER

Saturday night ended on a high note, and even though I didn't reveal myself, things were right on track for where I wanted them. Evangeline and I kissed for much longer than we should have, and when I finally pulled away Cole was gone. He didn't say anything, didn't try to stop us, just got dressed and left.

I texted him when I left to see where he took off to but no reply. After he didn't call me back this morning about playing some b-ball, I decided to go to his place to try to figure out what's going on. When he opens the door, he's got a beer in his hand and already looks like he's had two drinks too many.

"What's going on, bro?" I ask, nodding to the beer. It's only eleven in the morning and though I'm a fan of throwing a few back watching an early weekend football game, drinking this early alone only says one thing.

"Nothing, *bro*," he spits out.

"Can I come in?"

He pushes the door open, walking away not saying anything but allowing me to follow him in.

"What happened to you last night?"

"I was done. I got off and left."

"But you never leave without talking to who we were with."

"Well, you seemed to be taking care of that for me." He glares at me.

"Don't be an ass."

"Then don't hog the girl." He downs the beer in his hand and quickly grabs for another one.

"Are you kidding me right now? If anything, I've let you have more than your fair share of this girl."

"Fair share? She's more than a piece of ass."

I'm taken aback by his comment. Something else is going on here. "What's that supposed to mean?" I may have sex with random strangers, but I'm always respectful and never once treated a woman like a piece of ass, and he knows that.

"She's special. She's different."

Yeah? Tell me something I don't know, but hearing this come from him scares me. My fists clench, and I bite out through my teeth, "You don't even know her."

"But, I do."

"What do you mean, *you do*?" I yell.

He sets his beer down hard on the counter, mumbling *fuck* under his breath before blurting out, "She's my student. The one I told you about. Who I took to the concert the other day."

Nothing but red fuels my fire, and it takes every ounce of me to stop and take a deep breath, trying to clarify what I'm hearing. "What?"

"She also works at the law firm we partnered with on the case I'm working on, and we've been spending every day together."

"No," I grunt out through clenched teeth.

"I know it's supposed to be anonymous, but fuck, man." Cole shakes his head, looking down. "I want her. I want this. I'm going to ask her to quit the club and just be with me. I'm sitting here getting drunk trying to forget her, forget you kissing her, but I can't. She's infested my mind, and I'm fucking gone."

"No." I stand still, trying to take in deep breaths, but my lungs are stuck shut. He can't like her. She's mine.

"Fuck you, *no*. I can do whatever I want. I've gotten to know her outside of the club. I want more, and I'm going to get more. You haven't even fucked her, so what do you care?"

Blind rage seeps in, and I lunge at him, squeezing my hand into a fist and punching my best friend square in the jaw.

"What the fuck, Carter?" I hear him say as he scrambles to get up. I'm bigger in size, and I haven't been drinking, so I'm glad the stupid ass doesn't try to get up and fight back. Instead, he watches me walk out of his place, having no clue why it took everything in my power not to kill him right then.

After blowing off some steam at the gym, I headed to the hospital to see if I can get a rematch from Kyle, in total denial that an eleven-year-old is my only friend now it seems.

"Are you practicing without me?" I ask as I walk in, seeing him sitting on the floor playing the game.

He laughs, barely turning his attention away from the game. "I don't need practice. I'll still kick your butt."

I grab the extra beanbag and sit next to him, purposely knocking into him to mess him up. "Oops, sorry about that," I say, trying to hide my laugh.

"You know, you really do need a life," he teases.

"Shut it. Now hurry up and finish the game so we can get started."

Our game begins, but instead of playing with the same gusto he always does, his mood turns somber as he says, "My mom told me you know."

I try to act stupid, keeping my attention on the game. "Told you what? That you're gonna lose and my tally on the board is taking over?"

"No, Carter. What you told them."

I pause, dropping my head and the remote.

"You could have told me, you know?"

Knowing what this kid is up against is breaking my heart. If he doesn't find a donor soon, I hate to think what's going to happen. He's become my friend, the coolest guy I know, and he's only eleven. I turn to face him. "That's not my place."

"I'm gonna die, aren't I?"

"Not if I have a say about it. We have another drive coming up, so don't think like that."

Kyle has a rare form of Hodgkin's Lymphoma and is in need of a bone marrow transplant. Finding a match has been almost impossible, but we're holding out hope.

This donor drive we're planning can't come fast enough. I've spread the word to as many people I can in the City, putting fliers everywhere and talking to every doctor I knew. I can't think that this might be his last hope because I know we'll find someone.

He takes a deep breath, turning back to the game. "I'm okay if I do."

"Okay with what?"

"If I die. My parents always told me I was their miracle, so maybe that miracle was only meant to last for so long."

My heart hurts for him, and I pause the game, putting my hand on his shoulder. "Miracles are forever," I say before reaching over and engulfing the little guy in my arms.

Chapter 26

EVANGELINE

My Monday starts off with a bang. At the staff meeting between my firm and Cole's, we learned that the case has been called off. Apparently, all the digging Cole and I were doing scared one of the accusers, and she came out saying the whole thing was a lie. It's great for the client, but I must admit, I'm a little sad my first case ended this way, and now, I won't see Cole as much throughout the day.

In the meeting he kept his eyes turned down, never once looking in my direction. The vibe he's giving off is nothing I've experienced from him at all these past few weeks. As we leave the meeting, I grab his arm, slightly pulling him toward my office.

When I get a good look at him, his face explains why he's acting this way. Even though everything looks perfectly in place, his lip is split open on the side, and his jaw looks slightly bruised.

"What happened to you?" I ask.

"Ah, nothing." He blows it off, walking into my office with his briefcase.

"Okay, then why don't you tell me what's going on with you today?" He shrugs, not willing to talk, so I ask, "Then why did you leave on Saturday night the way you did?"

"Wait, who are we playing today? Co-workers? Professor/student? Or are we the people who've been fucking each other at the club?"

His tone pisses me off, and if he's ready for a fight, I'm more than ready to give him one. "Excuse me?" I say, crossing my arms over my chest.

"I'm just playing by your rules. I thought when we were here, at work, we acted like we didn't know who Maverick and, oh wait, *Evangeline*, are?"

My eyes grow big, and I'm right about ready to kick him out when he sighs. "Fuck. I'm sorry. That was wrong. It's just been a crazy couple of days."

"I don't care how your days have been. What gives you the right to step into my office and talk to me that way?"

"You're right. I just…" He pauses, walking closer to me. "I lost my shit on Saturday."

"So you take it out on me, on Monday, two days later?"

"I couldn't help it. I thought I could come in here and play the co-worker role with you, but one look at you and everything came back from Saturday night."

"What in the world are you talking about? If I remember correctly, I fucked you."

"But you didn't know it was me."

"Um, yeah, hello? It's an anonymous club. I shouldn't know it's you in the first place."

"Fuck," he mumbles under his breath, turning and walking around my office. "But you kissed him."

"Are you serious right now? You're pissed because while you had your dick in me, I kissed someone else?"

"Yes. No. Ahh," he growls. "I just don't know anymore. I've never been like this. With anyone." He turns around to look at me. "I like you, Evangeline."

I'm silent, not sure how to respond. I do have feelings for him, but I'm still not sure if I want to have these types of feelings for anyone. I turn around, hoping for a second to gather my thoughts without him staring at me.

He walks up behind me, placing his hands on my shoulders. "Please tell me you feel this too. Whatever is happening between us?"

"Cole…" I say, still not sure how to finish my sentence.

"Please don't go back to the club," he states.

"Excuse me?" I turn around to face him again.

"I don't want you there anymore. And I won't go either."

"Why?"

"Because I want you, Evangeline. I want to see where this goes, just the two of us. I told you I'd earn my right to be with you as a normal couple, and I really want to try."

"Cole…it's just…I mean…I don't know."

"It's him isn't it?"

"What? Who? Secret?"

"Fuck. Stop this Secret shit. It's him then. You like him yet you don't even know him. I watched the way you kissed him. But it's not him, it's the idea of him. What, are you too afraid of actual reality and would rather live behind the mask?"

"Get out," I demand.

"I will, but I'm not going anywhere. I don't know what your hang-ups are, but I want to be with you, and I can tell you like me too. Whatever issues you need to work through, fine. All I'm asking is that you work through them with me. Stop hiding and start living."

He walks out, slamming my door behind him, leaving me speechless.

I didn't go to class last night, but I couldn't help the unease in my stomach when I saw an email from Cole this morning. Clicking on it, I see that he only sent the notes I missed from class and nothing else. Never mentioning our conversation or anything about us. His email was strictly professor/student mode, and the idea ticked me off. We're so much more than that.

He's giving me space, but now that I have it, I'm even more confused on whether I even want it. He's right. About everything.

I do like him. I've enjoyed our time together more than I have with anyone in a long time. What he's asking isn't out of line, but I'm not ready to give up the club. I've only just begun, and I need to think some more before jumping into a relationship with the first person I meet there.

My cell rings, and I see Kamii's pretty face flash across the screen. "Hey, girl," I say into the phone.

"So, you want to tell me why I just got an email to the club saying that Cole is turning in his membership?"

"Did he really?"

"What's going on?"

"He asked me not to go anymore. He wants to date and see where we could go."

"And what did you say?"

I sigh. "We got in a fight, and he said I needed to stop hiding."

"Well, what do you think?"

I pause. Having to admit this out loud is harder than I thought. "He's right." I sit back in my seat, feeling defeated yet somewhat freed for admitting it. "He thinks I have feelings for this other guy but more just feelings for the unknown factor of him."

"Do you?"

"I don't even know the guy. I mean"—I bite my inner lip thinking back to that kiss—"I love the whole secret side of him. I'm not going to lie, it turns me on like no other not knowing anything about him. But then he kissed me..."

After a long pause, Kamii pipes in, "And…"

"There was just something different about his kiss. Cole said he noticed it too and got pissed when he saw me kissing him at the club."

"Angie, I don't want you staying in the club just for us. If you don't want to go anymore then that's totally fine."

Now I really feel bad. Through all my jumbled thoughts, I never once thought about the fact of why I was really there. For Kamii and Preston. To help them with the club, being the one person on the inside making sure things are running smoothly. How could I forget that fact? I can't leave.

"It's okay. I wouldn't leave anyway. I'm shocked he'd turn in his resignation so early. We just had that conversation yesterday. Maybe this is his way of telling me he's serious."

"But, Angie, he doesn't know who owns the club. He has no clue you'd find out this information. If he says he likes you and wants to try at a relationship, then he's telling the truth. Now you just need to decide what you want."

"Welcome back," I hear Cole say as I walk into the classroom.

After talking to Kamii, I thought for a long time about Cole and what I should do. Every time my email dinged I secretly wished it were him. Never was, though, beyond that one time about class notes.

When I saw him sitting at his desk, butterflies fluttered in my stomach, and I couldn't help the smile that pulled on my lips.

I do like him.

No matter how hard I fight it, those feelings are there, and now that I've gone a few days without him, they are there even more. He's worked his way into my life, into my heart and no matter how hard I fight it, sometimes fate has a mind of its own.

"Hello, Professor Spence. Sorry I missed Monday."

"No problem at all. I hope everything is okay."

I smile sweetly. "All better now."

The way his face lights up with my admission melts my heart, and I can't wait for the night to hurry up and get over with.

After class, I walk up to his desk and wait for my turn to talk to him. Sonia finishes her questions then glances in my direction before walking away.

"Thanks for the email. I appreciate your understanding of me not being able to make it on Monday."

"Of course. I'm sorry you had trouble in your real life. I hope everything is okay now."

I hear the click of the door closing, telling me that we're alone, and Cole wastes no time, jumping to his feet and pulling me into him.

"I'm sorry I was such a dick on Monday."

I look up into his eyes.

"I mean it. I was out of line. You have my head all fucked up, and I can't think straight when I'm around you."

I take a deep breath. "I'm not sure if I'm ready for this," I admit.

"It's okay, neither am I, but I'm ready to jump in and see where this goes." He pauses, moving my hair to the side and holding my hands. "Are you with me?"

I nod, looking up into his eyes, and instantly his lips touch mine, kissing me like he never has before.

Grabbing my hand in one hand, his bag in the other, he leads me out of the classroom.

"Where are we going?"

"To my place."

"What? Why?"

He stops, turning to me. "Because I've fucked you when it was just sex. Now it's more, and I want to show you what more is."

And he's right. This is more.

Chapter 27

COLE

My heart dropped when she entered my classroom. This girl has done me in, and if she was going to turn me down, I don't know how I could have gone on. The drive to my place is quiet but nice. There's no tension in the air or anticipation. Just a calmness I've always wanted with a girl and am shocked that I found it in her.

I wrap my hand around hers, smiling over at her, and I love the blush that runs up her face. How did I get so lucky to have her walk into my life in so many different ways? It's like it was fate, making sure no matter what we ended up together.

And yeah, I know I'm talking like a crazy man now, but fuck, this girl is everything. I'm going to make it my mission tonight to show her how different this can be and that she made the right choice to be with me.

She hasn't been to my place, and I'm praising the Lord I took the time to clean it last night. I was so antsy I couldn't keep still. Every part of me wanted to run to her door and beg her to forgive me. I knew if I were patient she'd come around, and I'm thankful she did so fast.

As we enter, I turn on the under-cabinet lights in the kitchen to give us enough glow to see but not enough to ruin the mood. If I had candles, I'd light them all over for her, but I don't want to scare her away. I can tell whatever happened in her past is heavy and until I know everything, I need to play every step safely.

"Can I get you something to drink?" I ask.

She looks around nervously. "Um, yeah, sure."

I walk up, grabbing her hands in mine. "You okay?"

She nods but doesn't answer.

"Just because you're here doesn't mean we're going to jump in and be together and live happily ever after."

She lets out a nervous laugh.

"One day at a time. We'll go slow and see where this goes," I try to reassure her.

My lips brush against hers, and I let go of her hands to run them through her hair, holding on to either side of her head. I feel her body give in, and I deepen the kiss, wanting more.

Within an instant, we're lost in each other, but I pull away, reaching for her hand again and winking as I walk her back to my bedroom. I could have taken her right there in my kitchen, but that's not what this is anymore. I want to show her the difference between fucking for a release and sex that actually means something.

Because it does; with this girl, it does mean something.

Moonlight shines through my window just enough to light the room in a blue tone, and it's perfect for our first meaningful time together outside of the club and trying to be something more, something real.

I sit on my bed and pull her hand into me, spreading my legs so she stands between them. My arms wrap around her waist, bringing her shirt up just enough to kiss her stomach. Her hands reach around my shoulders and hold on to my head. The light tug of her fingers in my hair reveals the slight tremble she has, so I wrap my arms around her tighter, letting her know I'm here, and there's no reason to be afraid.

Slowly, I move my hands higher, bringing her shirt with me, revealing her beautiful body with her black lace bra. Without a beat, I move to her pencil skirt, unzipping it from behind. I love when she comes to class straight from work with her sexy-as-sin, classy outfits.

Her hips shimmy side-to-side as I slide it down her toned legs and reach around to grip her bare ass firmly. My thumbs wrap around her thong, but I move in first, working my way down her stomach as I pull them off, kissing every place where the thin material used to be.

My eyes tilt up to her while I'm bent down, helping her to step out of her panties. I smirk and love that she instantly bites her lip, before reaching down to bring me back up and pull me into a kiss.

The moan that escapes her lips makes my hard cock start to ache in my jeans, and when her hands reach in to relieve the pressure, my body tingles from the pleasure of her soft fingers gripping me like she never has before.

At this moment, I know she feels the difference between us, and I swear my heart opens a little more as her tongue sweeps in to dance with mine.

The twinkle in her eye when she pulls back does me in even further, and when she looks down, starting to remove my clothes like I did to her, I realize I'm a done man.

Once I'm naked, I lean in to discard her bra and run my hands up and down her body before turning her around and laying her on the bed. I don't say anything, just because I don't want to ruin it. No cheesy words or dirty nonsense needs to be uttered right now. Everything I want her to know I can show her with my actions.

Laying my body on hers, I lean down to kiss her lips softly, working my way down her frame as I reach to my nightstand to grab a condom, and then slip it on while trying to still pay attention to her. I don't want protection to ruin our moment, but I'd never go without, at least not yet in our relationship. I can wait until she gives me that side too.

Positioning myself at her entrance, I kiss her lips as I slide inside, feeling her body tightly against mine, welcoming me in. The moan releasing from her mouth tells me I'm entering more than her body, but her heart too.

I don't focus on different positions or only sticking my dick in to get off. No. For the first time, I take it all and give it right back. Every touch, every kiss, every pulse means something, and I don't miss the way her head falls back or how her hands grip my back, trying to pull me in closer to her.

What we have is something special, and for this one moment, I never want it to end. I'll make it my life's mission to make this girl mine. This, right here, is what I want to have for the rest of my life.

When her body tightens, so close to her release, I push a little harder, slowing down each thrust until I hear her scream and her body clenches around mine. The feeling is all I need to let go and grunt out a new me with every thrust.

Now, having her wrapped in my arms is the best feeling in the world. I play with her hair as I say, "Thank you for giving me a chance." Her fingers play with the hair on my chest, and I grab them, bringing them up to my lips and kissing them softly.

Her bracelet falls down, and something I've never noticed on her catches my attention. For a brief second my world stops. The thin line tattoo on the inside of her wrist is one I've seen many times and had many conversations about, only not with her. Memories of Carter on Sunday run through my mind, and instantly, my blood starts to boil.

There's no fucking way.

Her head is lying on my chest, so I try to still my breathing and not bring any attention to my thoughts. There are so many questions I have, but one thing's for sure. She can never go to the club again.

Chapter 28

EVANGELINE

"Um, Angie…can you give me a call when you get this?" Kamii's voice says when I check my message. Her voice is peculiar and instantly rubs me the wrong way, so I call her back quickly.

"Oh, good, you got my message," Kamii says as her greeting.

"Yeah, you got my nerves working. What's up?" I hate when people leave cryptic messages like this. It gets my stomach working in ways that no one enjoys.

"So, you're never going to believe what email I got today."

"You're killing me, you know that? What?"

"Cole."

"Okay…does he want back in?"

"No, opposite actually. He wants your secret guy kicked out."

"What?" I jump up from my seat, so many thoughts instantly running through my mind. "Why?"

We've just spent the night together. I told him I'd give us a try. I'm so confused.

"He's accusing him of being forceful with a member."

"He is not! Why would he do that?"

My mind starts to go crazy. This makes no sense. Secret was anything but forceful. I thought they were friends. Is there something I don't know? Thoughts of something happening after I left his place start to run wild in my mind.

"That's why I'm calling you. What happened with you two?"

"This makes no sense. We made up, and I even went to his house last night. We didn't talk about it, but I thought it was pretty obvious that I'm willing to try the whole relationship thing with him."

"You are?" she interrupts.

"Well, I was. But this…I don't get it. This is overstepping boundaries. I didn't plan on going, but now I want to just to spite him."

This is exactly why I don't date. I don't need drama in my life. I've had enough for three lifetimes already. What could he have possibly done to deserve Cole stabbing him in the back like this?

"But, Angie," Kamii speaks again. "He doesn't know you're involved in the workings of the club and that you'd find out he's turning him in."

"Ah!" I scream out. I totally forgot about that fact. "That's even worse. He's going behind my back, and that's not okay. This is the real him. I can't be with someone who'd do something like this, to a friend at that. And for what? He already has me. Is he that concerned I'd go to him?"

"He must be."

"This. This is why I don't do relationships. I'll show him. His actions are about to backfire on his ass, and there's not a damn thing he can do about it."

"So you're going to go tonight?"

"Hell yeah, I am. I guess this will go down as the quickest relationship I've ever had. Do what you want with the email, but know that he's full of crap."

We hang up, and my blood feels like it's boiling through my veins. I'm so confused, so frustrated, but above all, ready to show him who's really boss. Nobody messes with me.

Anger fuels my fire tonight. This is the biggest *fuck you* to Cole, and I can't wait to see the look on his face when I tell him about it tomorrow and that we're done. I won't have a man stake his claim on me like this. There's no reason for him to kick him out, and I'm going to make sure he knows he screwed up big time.

I dress in my sexiest outfit, ready to knock the socks off this guy and get back to the reason why I joined the club in the first place; the fact that there's no personal connection.

Just sex. Nothing else.

Cole is supposed to be coming to my house tonight, but he's going to get the surprise of his life when he finds a note on my door saying I'm here. Oh, but guess what? Since he turned in his resignation, he can't get in, and the bouncers have strict orders not to let him in for any reason.

When I walk in, I see Secret standing at the bar, looking straight at the door, like he's waiting for me to walk in. His lips pull up into a smirk, and my anger turns to excitement, knowing I'm finally going to get him tonight.

I go straight to him. "Do I get to know your name yet?"

He shakes his head.

"Are you going to talk tonight?"

He shakes his head again.

"Good. Follow me."

This will be perfect.

He pauses, looking around like he's searching for Cole, and I turn to him. "He's not coming tonight. It's just you and me. Are you okay with that?"

His smile lights up what I can see of his face as he nods and continues walking to our spot, this time taking the lead.

Lightly touching my arms, he guides me to the bed where he drops to his knees. After running his fingers down my arms until he's holding my hands, he brings them up to his mouth and kisses each one.

Placing them on my sides, he leans in, quickly pressing his lips to mine before moving down my neck, over my cleavage, down my waist until he's kissing his way down my legs to remove each shoe.

Leaning back, he carefully removes his shirt, and for the first time, I get to see the muscles that make up this mysterious man. Every line and every curve are carefully constructed, telling me he either spends hours at a gym or is in some kind of construction. When he runs his fingers up my legs again, I know it's not the latter.

My body falls back against the bed, feeling what he's doing to me. His hands are soft yet firm. I can feel the roughness from where a weightlifting bar would leave a mark but not where it tells me he uses his hands for manual labor. The way they rub over my body, like he's on his knees, worshiping over me, is something I haven't felt in years. Not since—*No!*

I push the idea out of my head and focus on the now. My head tilts to the side where I can view another scene going on and the sight fuels my fire more. I'm not here for this kind of sex. I'm here to fuck.

Bringing myself back up, I reach down to unzip his pants, ready to get this party going. He stops me, though.

"Let's not rush," he whispers out in the same harsh voice.

Right at this second, for the first time, the voice doesn't turn me on and him saying not to rush actually frustrates me.

Taking a deep breath, I look over at the scene again, trying to change my mood and rid my brain of my sudden thoughts of the past.

His hands grip my waist, lifting them up slightly before slowly removing my panties, in what feels like one centimeter at a time. He's going so slowly like he's savoring each second, and I'm starting to go insane. I'm here for a release, nothing else.

I release my bra, trying to move things along, but nervous, with the attitude I've found myself in, if he grabs my nipples the way men like to do I might explode. I'm not in the mood for that and sometimes wish I could just come out and say this is what I like and what I don't like before I even kiss a guy.

The gods must be looking down on me because to my amazement, he doesn't even touch my nipples. Instead, he grips my entire breast underneath, softly kneading it with his hands and licking everywhere except there. It's been years since I've enjoyed my breasts being played with, and I drop my head back, praising this guy for helping to bring me out of my funk.

When his lips finally reach mine, a familiarity rings through my body and within an instant, I'm lost in his lips, wanting him more now than I've ever wanted anything in my entire life. The surge running through me lights my soul on fire, and I only want more.

Finally, he allows my hands to unbuckle his pants and slide them down his legs, revealing a lower half that rivals his upper half.

Our lips stay locked in a passionate kiss while he holds me tightly with one hand and runs his fingers through my hair with the other. I feel so alive, so secure in his arms and for a brief moment, it's not until I hear the cries from someone in another scene that I remember where we are.

Pulling back, I try to regain my sense of *this is just fucking*, while he kisses his way down my stomach again. Once the condom he reached for from the table is secure, he still doesn't push inside.

Instead, he runs his fingers over my stomach, almost as if he's searching for something. When he finds the small stretch mark I have hidden on my hip, he leans down, softly kissing it before sliding inside me. He reaches his arms around my body, holding me tightly and slowly pulling in and out.

Everything feels different. This is nothing like what I've felt in this club, yet it's everything I've wanted for so long. The way his body molds to mine, the way I can feel his heart beat and his breath on my neck, the way he's holding on to me like he can't believe I'm here, and what surprises me the most is the way I'm holding him back.

My emotions run wild with every purposeful pulse he makes. I never want this to end, but I feel the deep burn building low, and I know there's no way to stop it, no matter how much I fight it. This man has taken complete control of my body, and I'm a slave to his touch.

My heart starts to pound as my breathing becomes more erratic, and when he pushes me over the edge, my body clenches around his and to my complete amazement, he stops. He thrusts once more inside me then holds it there, waiting for me to ride my wave and feel every ounce of release his body just gave me.

It's perfect, it's what I want every guy to do when I cum, it's what—

No. No. No. There's no way.

"It is me," he whispers in my ear, answering the question flying through my brain, and I jump up, trying to push him off me.

He moves, and I push myself back on the bed, but he doesn't let me get too far. He grabs my wrist and turns it over, revealing my tattoo. I sit, frozen in fear, as he removes his thick watch, uncovering his matching one.

"It's me, Evangeline," he says in his real voice, and I gasp in recognition.

I always loved the way he said my name and knowing I'd never hear it again is another reason why I changed it to Angie. Hearing it now, though, I've never been so lost, so scared, so completely out of my mind that I don't know what to do.

So I do what I know best.

I run.

I run naked to the exit, grabbing my wrap dress and running out, not even bothering to look for my shoes.

"Evangeline, stop!" Cole yells from the open door of his car as he runs after me outside the club.

"No. Go away, Cole!" I yell as I run down the street to where I'm parked, still pulling together my dress.

The bouncer runs after me as well. "Sir, you need to back off," he yells to Cole.

I reach my car and turn to see Cole twenty feet away holding his hands up, saying, "Evangeline, talk to me. I just want to make sure you're okay."

"This is all your fault!" I yell back.

"Sir," the bouncer warns, and Cole takes another step back.

"What did I do? Talk to me," Cole begs.

"I had no intention of coming back to this club. I was willing to give us a go. To only be with you. But you went and fucked up. You pushed me to come back."

"What are you talking about?" he yells.

"I would have never come back. I would have never known. I didn't want to know," I cry out, falling to my knees in front of my car.

"Know what?" Cole plays dumb, but if only he knew how really fucked up this is.

"About me," Carter yells out as he calmly walks around the corner.

Cole looks at Carter who, for the first time, doesn't have his mask on, and I see it. It's really him. He's changed a lot. Much bigger and his head is close shaven, but deep down, I know it's him.

The bouncer looks around, trying to figure out the situation.

Carter tries to run to me, but the bouncer stops him. "I don't think so," he says.

"I need to talk to her," Carter announces.

"You need to stay away," Cole demands.

"What the fuck, Cole? You don't know? This is her. The girl I've talked about for all these years."

"I know!" he yells back.

"You knew?" I scream out. "How could you possibly know? Oh my God, that's why you tried to kick him out of the club."

"You tried to kick me out?" Carter questions Cole. "What the fuck, man?"

"I was just trying to protect her."

"From what? From me?"

"Yes, from you. Obviously, she ran from you for a reason."

Carter lunges at Cole. "You knew what she meant to me. You knew how long I've searched for her."

The bouncer runs to them, pulling Carter off him after he gets in a few punches.

"Stop!" I scream at the top of my lungs. "Both you of you, just stop." I open my door. "I don't ever want to see either of you, ever again!"

"Evangeline," they both yell, but the bouncer stops them from getting any closer to me.

"Let her go," he demands, towering over both of them, daring them to try anything.

And I do. I go. I just don't know where yet.

Chapter 29

CARTER

I knew she'd freak out, but I didn't think she'd have that drastic of a response. I ran after her, but when I saw Cole standing there, waiting, I froze, not sure what was going on. Why the hell would he be there, and outside the club at that?

Something else is going on, and as I sat there, listening to their exchange, I heard my worst fears. I knew he liked her, but hearing that she was willing to give up the club to be in a relationship with him gutted me.

But when I heard he tried to get me kicked out of the club all I saw was red. Cole's been my one friend, the guy who knows everything and has been there through it all. The first four years after we split I spent looking for her but never thought about the baby.

It wasn't until I moved to San Francisco that I started looking into anything I could do legally to know where my baby is, and Cole is the one who helped me.

I poured my heart out to him many times and to hear him stab me in the back like that pushed me over the edge, and friends or not, I wanted to kill him.

Thank God, the bouncer was there to stop me, and Cole was smart, getting in his car and leaving. The only shitty thing is he probably followed

Evangeline, and here I am, sitting outside the club like an asshole since I left the keys to my car inside, along with my wallet and shoes.

The bouncer stares at me like I've done something wrong, but dealing with him is the last of my worries, so without saying anything, I walk back to the entrance, grab my stuff and head out.

I know I'll be hearing about this. There's no way they'd allow someone to leave this club that upset and not try to figure out why.

The City may only be seven square miles, but when you're driving around aimlessly searching for one car, in particular, it may as well be a million.

After an hour, I finally realize it's hopeless, so I drive to Cole's place. When I don't see his car, rage fills me again.

He has to be with her.

Without thinking I call him, ready to light his ass up, even if it's on his voicemail, but when he answers, I wasn't expecting what I heard.

"She's gone. What the fuck did you do?"

"What did I do? What did you do?"

"Fuck, Carter. You need to back off. I really like this girl, and she was giving us a shot."

I laugh. "A shot? You're kidding me, right? You knew who she was to *me*," I yell, "yet you were going to try to keep her from me?"

"Yes, I was. I'll admit it. She left you years ago, and now it's my turn."

"Your turn?" My voice gets even louder, astonished to hear what's coming out of his mouth. "She gave birth to *my* child."

"Yeah, that she gave up and never told you about. Or did you forget?"

"Fuck you."

"Right back at you," he demands before hanging up the phone, leaving me no closer to finding her.

EVANGELINE

I couldn't go home, I knew that much. Cole knew where I lived, and I needed to be away from him right now. I couldn't go to my friends' house because how in the world would I even begin to tell them how fucked up things have gotten.

So I turned to the only person I knew who would understand, and, more importantly, where I could speak freely about what just went down.

My tears faded when I saw the rage that Carter and Cole had toward each other but when Kamii opened her front door, they came again in full strength, and I had to hold on to the railing to keep myself from falling to the ground.

"Angie, what happened?" she asks, running out to catch me and hold me tightly.

I feel bad knocking on her door like this, but I turned off my phone as soon as I got in my car, so I couldn't call to give her a heads-up I was coming over. I didn't want to risk seeing Cole calling me, so instead of having to ignore it, I shut it down completely.

"It's him," I cry out, gasping for air through my tears, unable to say anything else.

"Who's him?" she asks, moving my hair away from my face.

"The guy I told you about the other day."

The look on her face almost makes me laugh. She's putting two and two together, and I'm waiting for her ah-ha moment to hit. Her eyebrows pinch together, and she says, "That you dated from high school?"

I nod, letting the tears flow heavier down my face.

"Warroad is the father of your son?"

"Warroad?" I say in disbelief. "Is that his club name?"

Of course, she knew this entire time what his club name was. The thought makes me ill. If she had just slipped once, or if I found his paperwork on accident when we were going over club business. I can't even imagine what I would have done.

"Yes. Why? Does it mean something to you?"

I shake my head in shock. That's why he never wanted me to know his club name. "Yes, it's the town we grew up in," I whisper out.

My legs get weak, and I fall fully into her arms. She holds me tightly and walks me into her house, guiding me to the couch where she sits me down and holds me into her chest.

I cry till I have nothing left.

"Did you really not know it was him?" she asks softly, I'm sure in the same shock I am about the entire situation.

"I know, right?" I sit back, wiping my tears. "But, ugh, he's changed a lot. I mean *a lot*. In high school, he was on the skinny side. He never lifted weights. I told you, more of a book nerd. Now he's built with muscles almost twice the size they were back then. He shaves his head now too where he always wore it longer back home. And remember how I told you he spoke differently like he was trying to disguise his voice? Well, now I know why. He must have known the entire time."

The thought makes me sit up straighter, suddenly pissed. "Shit. He knew the entire time! His mask, it covered most of his face and, *fuck*, he got a new one right after the night I first met him. He knew! How could he do this to me?"

Images of all of our times together flash through my head, and now I'm more pissed at myself. Here I thought he was playing a game, being secretive to make my experience more exciting, and the whole time he was only playing me for a fool. I was so stuck on the excitement of not knowing who he was that I didn't see past his façade.

"I feel so stupid," I say, burying my face in my hands.

Kamii reaches out to me. "No, sweetie, don't say that. You didn't know, and for some reason, he didn't want you to. At least not then."

I bite my lip, looking up at the ceiling, trying not to cry again.

"So how did you finally find out?"

"It was his game. Shit." I stop, shaking my head as I think back to us being together. "He was dropping hints left and right. He wanted me to figure out it was him."

"So did you or did he say something?"

I look up at her, tears forming in my eyes again. "I did."

Kamii's arms wrap around me again. I can't believe I knew it was him just by his touch. Shit, by his kiss. That's why I'd get so lost. Even Cole saw it, but I didn't want to acknowledge it then.

"Wait, but I forgot to tell you about Cole," I say, throwing the pillow off me that I grabbed for comfort when I first sat down.

"He wasn't there tonight, right? He wasn't on the list, so he shouldn't have been," she confirms.

"No. He wasn't, but he was waiting outside. But that's not what I'm getting at. He knew."

"He knew what?"

"He knew Carter and I had a past. That's why he was trying to get him kicked out. So I wouldn't figure out who he was."

Anger fills me again, and I stand up, not able to sit anymore.

"Holy schmoly!" Kamii says in shock.

"There was a scene outside the club, and the bouncer had to pull the two of them off each other after I asked Cole why he'd do that."

"Angie..." She stands up to hug me again.

I take a few deep breaths, letting her embrace me, calm me down, and bring me back to reality. Even though I have no idea what my reality even is now.

"Can I stay here tonight?" I finally ask when I pull away.

"Of course, sweetie."

"Cole knows where I live, and I can't face him tonight," I admit, embarrassed I have nowhere else to go.

"You can stay as long as you want. I'll go get some blankets for the spare room then we'll get that pint of ice cream from the fridge and binge. Sound good?"

I let out a small laugh. "Please. I can't thank you enough," I say, stopping her before she walks to the kitchen.

"Anytime. I'm glad you came here. Shoot, I need the ice cream probably more than you do." She winks.

I love that she's trying to change my mood. Instantly, I know this is exactly where I need to be.

Chapter 30

EVANGELINE

It helps to be friends with my boss. I was due for some vacation time anyway, and Kamii was able to get me some time off to deal with my emotions. I cried for a few days and sulked for the others, finally coming to the conclusion that I need to face my past.

When I left Minnesota, I promised myself I'd never go back, yet here I am, on a plane, about to face my worst fears. When Kamii first suggested I go home, I thought she was crazy, but I finally broke down and contacted Kaitlyn. We both cried and then talked for hours about everything, and by the end of the conversation, I was ready to pay her a visit.

I have to fly into Minneapolis, and it's a six-hour drive to Warroad. I was even more excited for the trip when Kaitlyn said she'd come pick me up. Being able to talk to her for that time, alone, will help ease me back into coming home.

After the plane lands, I turn on my phone to text her that we've landed. Of course, there's also a text from Cole, but I don't read it. Not yet.

He's texted or called every day, but I haven't read or listened to any messages. I can only handle one thing at a time right now. His persistence is surprising me, though.

When I walk out, I see Kaitlyn jumping up and down when her eyes meet mine. She and I were two peas in a pod, both crazy as hell and loving every minute.

I run to her, for the first time not nervous at all about coming home. My soul needed this to both heal and move on.

We scream like little girls with both of us letting tears fall down our faces.

"It's so good to see you. I've missed you so much," I say, squeezing her tight.

"You too! I can't believe you're actually here."

She helps me with the carry-on I brought on the plane, and we head to her car, getting ready for our trip back to Warroad.

"God, I'm just in shock right now. It's been too long," she says as she gets on the freeway.

"It has. How have you been?"

"Not much has changed here. The second round of kids is happening with our friends, and we even have our first divorce. But even we knew back in high school that Eric was gay, so that's no surprise."

"He finally came out?"

"Yup. Shelly acted all surprised, but she must have been in blind denial if she never knew. The new gossip is that he's dating Max, though." She eyes me in amazement.

"No!" I say in disbelief. "The quarterback from the year before us?"

"That's the one! He's dated just about every single girl in town, but now we know why none ever lasted."

"Well, good for them. Everyone deserves to find their special someone."

"What about you then? Have you found that special someone?"

I sigh, dropping my head back. When we spoke on the phone, I didn't tell her anything about what was really going on. I knew I'd have to, but the thought fills my eyes with tears.

"Oh, Evangie," she calls me by the nickname she always has. "What's going on?"

"It's almost so unbelievable it's hard for even me to fathom."

"You can tell me. You know I'm here."

"I know. It's Carter," I admit and she swerves the car, over-correcting to the other side, and I grip the door handle when she steadies the vehicle back to a straight line.

"How did he find you? Or, holy shit, did you contact him?"

"Well—"

She interrupts, "He's looked everywhere for you, for many years."

"Really?" I ask, surprised.

"Are you kidding me? He was frantic about it. I honestly thought at one point he was going to drop out of school to search the world for you."

Guilt takes me over, and I drop my head, blinking away the tears I don't want to fall.

"So what happened?" she continues, I'm sure feeling guilty for bringing my disappearance up at all. "How did he find you?"

"That's the funny thing. We found each other."

"What? How?"

"God. I told you it's unbelievable." I look over at her, and she raises her eyebrows, egging me on. "We ran into each other at an anonymous sex club."

"Shut up!" she yells. "Okay, I'm going to hear a lot more about this club, but first, how in the world?"

I cover my eyes. "Don't judge. I've had a long ten years, and the last thing I wanted was a relationship. So when I got the opportunity to join the club I jumped on it."

"Ha, literally," she interrupts, and I laugh out loud.

"So, what, you recognized him? What's the anonymous part?"

"You wear masks, and I guess he knew it was me right away, but he did everything in his power to make sure I didn't know it was him."

"Okay, seriously, how did you not know?"

"Have you seen pictures of him?"

She nods, thinking about it. "Yeah, I guess he has changed a lot."

"A lot? That's the understatement of the year."

"Well, yeah, I guess from high school he's changed a ton. I've seen him every so often, so I haven't thought about just how much, but yeah, thinking back to high school he was a little scrawny back then."

"He comes home a lot?"

"Yeah, I guess every few months. Whenever he can. He's supporting his parents. You know that, right?"

"No!" I admit.

"Yup. His mom had a stroke a few years back. She's doing okay now, but she hasn't worked since. He sends them money and even moved them into a different house so she can move around easier."

Of course he did. He's always been such an amazing guy and hearing this doesn't surprise me at all.

I'm silent as I let the thought of him sink in.

Kaitlyn breaks through my thoughts. "So continue, sex club you were saying? I need to make it out to see you. San Francisco sounds like my kind of place." She winks, and I laugh.

She'd die to see such a large city with so many people around. I don't think she's left Warroad much, and the shock might be too much for her to take in.

"So yeah. I figured out who he was but not until I'd already fallen for his friend."

"What?" She jumps in her seat, holding on to the steering wheel in shock before looking at me.

"It's a mess, Kaitlyn. But the worst part is I still haven't spoken to him."

"Which one?"

I look at her in disbelief. "Carter!"

"You haven't spoken to him about what?" She tiptoes around what I know she really wants to ask, but we're nowhere near that question, not yet.

"About anything." I sigh. "I found out it was him and ran." I look over at her, waiting for her disapproval, but it never comes.

"So when was this?"

"A week ago…?"

She turns her head to me and back to the road as she tries to figure everything out. "Let me get this straight. You found him—or rather he found you—at a sex club I might add, and you guys still haven't spoken?"

I pull at the hem of my shirt, hating when I admit, "No. I don't know what to do. What can I do?"

"About what?"

I whisper out, "About everything. It's been so long, too long. Too much has happened."

"But none of that matters. It's all in the past," she says like it's no big deal.

"But is it? There's so much to tell him but how do I—"

"He knows," she interrupts, gripping the steering wheel and not looking at me.

My head falls and tears instantly fall freely. "How?"

She looks at me, taking a deep breath. "Evangeline, you left. You took off, and I was so worried about you. So scared for months, shit, years. Don't hate me, but I told him."

My head falls back against the headrest as we sit in silence for a few seconds. I turn to look at her. "I could never hate you."

"I was just worried about you. I thought he needed to know."

"How did he react?"

She lets out a sigh. "Let's just say there were multiple times I wished I hadn't told him."

"I'm sorry I put you in that position."

She shrugs, blowing it off. "I can't blame you. I don't know what I'd do in that situation, so I'm not one who can judge. Do you mind me asking what you did? With no mention of a child traveling with you, did you…?"

I bite my lip before answering, "We had a boy. I gave him up for adoption."

She reaches over, squeezing my hand. "You know that's the ultimate motherly sacrifice, right?"

I shake my head slightly. "You're the second person to tell me that this week."

"Well, it's true. You knew you couldn't give him a good life, so you found someone who could. I'm proud of you."

"I'm sure Carter doesn't feel the same way."

"Hey, everything happens for a reason. You guys weren't meant to be parents yet. He needed to get his degree and save lives. He would have quit and come back."

"See, that's what I didn't want."

"I know. I totally get it. And I know without a doubt he would have. I can't say keeping it from him was right, but I'm saying I understand where you were coming from."

I smile at her, silently thanking her for agreeing with my logic from so many years ago.

Chapter 31

EVANGELINE

"Life hasn't changed much around here," Kaitlyn says as we walk down Main Street, heading to my favorite burger joint growing up.

"I forgot how beautiful it was, though," I say, looking around and taking a deep breath of fresh air.

She stops, confused. "Beautiful? It's just Main Street."

Laughing, I reply, "Yes, but the streets are clean, and I don't have to worry about stepping in a bum's pee as I walk down the sidewalk. And the air, my God, I forgot how good trees smell."

"You're not serious, right?"

"I wish I could say I wasn't. San Francisco is not the cleanest place on the Earth. It's more like the concrete jungle you hear people talk about."

"But bums' pee?"

I almost snort my reply. "Sometimes I wish pee was the only thing I had to deal with when it came to bums. You name it, I've seen it, and it's not pretty."

"Okay, I'm beginning to think Warroad isn't all that bad."

"No, it really isn't," I reply as we walk into my childhood heaven.

I always loved this place. It was where my parents took me to celebrate my birthdays or when I aced my tests in school. For the first time in years, I don't feel that punch in the gut whenever I think about them.

I order the same thing I always did, a plain cheeseburger with a side of mac n' cheese, and I'd always put the mac n' cheese on the burger to eat them together. It sounds disgusting everywhere else, but here, it's comfort food.

I talk to a few people I haven't seen in years but nothing could have prepared me for the surprise I got halfway through our meal. Kaitlyn and I were reminiscing about shenanigans we used to get into when I heard the doorbell chime upon opening. Without realizing why, I glanced in their direction to see Carter's parents.

His mom meets my eyes first, and a small smile appears on her face with a slight tilt to her head. She grabs her husband's arm, leaning over to say something, causing him to look in my direction too. He nods his head, following the hostess to their seats, but she heads our way instead.

I glance at Kaitlyn, who has her eyebrows raised, and she widens her eyes to me when she notices this is about to go down. They weren't all that fond of me in high school, and now, I have no clue if they know about the child I gave up; their grandson.

"Evangeline," his mom, Judy, says in the sweetest manor as she approaches my table.

Kaitlyn chokes on her food and instantly coughs into her napkin as I say, "Hi, Judy. Long time no see."

"Yes, darling, it has been a long time. How have you been?"

Okay, she's being nice to me. This is a first. "I'm good. How about you guys?"

"We're hanging in there. I talked to Carter last week, and he had mentioned he found you."

I'm so glad I just swallowed the drink I had taken, or I would have spat it out directly on her. Coughing to clear my throat, I respond, "He did?"

"Yes, honey, he did. He's been looking for you for years, you know?"

I turn to Kaitlyn, not sure how much she knows about everything.

"I can't help but feel responsible too," she finishes.

"Um," I say because I have no clue how else to respond.

"I'm sorry. I was never terribly nice to you," she says, reaching down to grab my hand, squeezing it lightly.

I stay silent again, still in some state of shock.

"I knew he really liked you, and I was so scared he'd give up his future for a high school fling. Then after your parents passed away and you disappeared, I've been carrying this guilt around. I knew you really needed him then, and I couldn't help but feel I was the reason you ran away."

Her apology does feel nice, but I still have no idea what to say.

"Well," she says, letting go of my hand. "I just wanted to tell you that. And I'm sorry about your parents. I know it's been a while, but I still think of them every time I drive past your old house."

Words finally escape my lips. "Thank you, Judy. I really appreciate your apology. It was a long time ago." I try to blow it off.

"Well, I'm glad to hear you're doing so well, and I hope you keep in touch with Carter. I know he'd really like that. Enjoy your visit while you're here."

"Thank you. It was good to see you."

"You too, hon."

She smiles at Kaitlyn and turns to leave us alone, my nerves and emotions a total wreck all over again.

I've been back home for a few days, enjoying the overload of memories I've had running into old friends and hanging out at the lake, enjoying the sun. But I leave tomorrow, and there's one place I have to visit before I go home.

Kaitlyn said she'd come with me, but this is something I have to do on my own. I've only seen pictures of my parents' gravestone and seeing it in real life makes me feel like for the first time I have some kind of closure.

Memories of how many nights I've begged for one more day with them and now that I'm standing here, a sense of peace overwhelms me. I've felt their presence the entire time I've been back, and now that I'm at their grave, I feel them even more. It's a feeling I've felt for many years yet I've never understood until now.

The feeling that I'm not alone is something I can never describe. All these years I've felt I had no one yet it was me who made it that way. I've reconnected with all my friends, their parents, and even new people. Every person treated me like no time has passed, and I'm still the same person I was.

And for the first time I feel like Evangeline again.

I turn to walk back to my car but am stopped in my tracks when I see a man sitting with his back to me on a bench. The sun has started to go down, so his sunglasses are sitting backward on his head, cuffed around his ears and balancing on his neck, something only one person I know ever did.

Carter.

I always teased him for wearing them that way, and I see that some things haven't changed. I should be freaking out, I should be nervous to talk to him, but the calmness I've just felt tells me it's time. It's time to face my past and to finally face him.

Slowly, I walk up and sit next to him. Both of us look straight out on the makeshift pond they created at the cemetery, not saying a word.

I feel his hand move, and when I look down, I see that he's holding it open, offering for me to take it in mine, and I accept. Wrapping my hand in his, we share this quiet moment that should have happened ten years ago.

A tear slips out of my eye as I whisper, "I'm sorry."

He shakes his head but still doesn't look at me. "Don't be. I'm the one who should be sorry." His head tilts down to his chest, and he grips my hand tighter. "I should have been there for you."

"But I'm the one who ran. Not you."

"Doesn't matter. I put you in that situation, and I've had to live with that for this past decade. If I hadn't left. If I had been more careful. If I hadn't gotten you pregnant, you wouldn't have run. You wouldn't have been alone."

"No, Carter. Those were all my decisions."

He turns to me, and his eyes are red with tears he's fighting back. "But I would have been there for you. We could have gone through it together."

"I know you would have. There was never a doubt in my mind that you would have come back. That's why I left. I didn't want you to give up what you worked so hard for."

"We could have figured something out. I don't know, I could have gotten some kind of off-campus housing. There were these—"

I stop him. There's no reason to dwell on what we could have done. "We had a boy."

He takes a sharp inhale in. I lift my other hand that's not wrapped in his to wipe my tears. "He was eight pounds, two ounces. I researched and met with multiple families to choose him the best one I could."

His head falls down again as his shoulders tremble.

"I get letters from them often, but I've never opened one. It didn't feel right without you by my side. I think I'm ready, though. To open them."

The most caring eyes I've ever seen meet mine with shock and excitement shining through. His arm reaches out to pull me in close to him. "I'd love to read them," he whispers, kissing my forehead.

With my head on his shoulder, we both sat in silence, staring out at the water, holding each other till the moonlight was all we saw.

Chapter 32

EVANGELINE

"You're cold," Cater states, rubbing my arms and bringing me closer to him after we sat on the bench in silence for a little while. This was exactly what I needed. For the first time in years, I could finally breathe. I didn't feel that sharp pain deep in my gut or the weight that constantly felt like I couldn't hold my shoulders up high.

I finally felt like me.

Carter always understood why sometimes I needed my quiet time and sitting here with him felt just as comfortable as it would be if I were sitting by myself.

I didn't want this moment to end, but he's right, the tank top and shorts I have on aren't offering the warmth I need from the summer breeze that's cutting through my thin T-shirt.

"Here, I'll take you home. I didn't see a car down at the parking lot. Did you walk here?"

I nod, biting my inner lip, scared to say anything. I've lived so long without him. I have so much to tell him and have no clue where to start, or even if we can start.

I mean, start what? With us? Are we an us? Does everything pick up where we left off? Where we are now? I have no clue.

He stands up and offers his hand out to me. Tilting his head to the side with a small smile on his face, he says, "Come on."

I grab his hand, letting him guide me up, so we're standing directly in front of each other. I can't help myself, and I wrap my arms around him. Pulling him in close to me, breathing in his scent, and loving the comfort I feel wrapped in his warmth.

My hands run down his arms, feeling the skin beneath his shirt along with the dips and valleys in his muscles. "Where the hell did these come from?" I tease.

He smirks. "Let's just say I spent a lot of time in the gym working off my frustrations."

"So…you're welcome then?" I ask, with a lift to my eyebrows and tilt to my lips, making sure what I said is okay. I know the frustrations he talks about revolve around not being able to find me.

Thankfully, he gets my joke and leans in to hug me. "I guess you're right. I should thank you for that."

"Well, it looks good on you."

Laughing, he grabs my hand and tugs me away from the bench and toward the parking lot.

We end up talking until the sun rises, sitting in his car in front of Kaitlyn's place. Holding on to him in silence at the pond was amazing but actually talking to him was even better.

He filled me in on how he got his degree and then the opportunity to be a pediatric oncologist at UCSF, while I filled him in on the crazy things I've done that led to working at the law firm.

We didn't talk about us, or about Cole, or even about our son. All of that can wait. We were just two friends catching up with one another, and it was perfect.

Kaitlyn told him what flight I was on, so we both leave today, which worked out great since he has to head home for a donor drive they are holding for one of his patients.

At seven, we finally said our goodbyes so I could pack, and he could go visit his parents for a few hours before he picks me up for the flight.

"Hey, look who's home," Kaitlyn says from the couch as she holds her coffee cup close to her body like she's guarding the liquid gold with her life.

"Carter showed up at the cemetery," I admit.

"I know. I hope you're not mad I told him where you were."

I plop down on the couch next to her. "Nah, I'm not mad. I guess I should actually thank you."

"Yeah?" She sits up, excited for some news about us.

"Nothing happened, don't get too excited," I say, throwing a pillow in her direction.

"Yeah, but you guys talked. That's huge. I know you don't like to hear it, but he really was a wreck over you. I felt so sorry for the guy."

"He told me." I sigh. "I think he understood why I did it, though."

"Of course he did. We've talked about it. He understood then, but that doesn't mean he was happy about it. He was just scared something had happened to you. We all were."

I look over at her, ready to apologize again, but she stops me. "Hey, none of that matters anymore. You're here. He's there. And you guys found each other. So what's the next step?"

"Who knows..." I sink down onto the couch more, resting my head against the back. "We're heading home in a few hours."

"Do you think you'll get back together with him? Wait, didn't you mention something about his best friend?"

I drop my head to my chest. Cole.

I was so wrapped up with being home, then talking to Carter again that I almost completely forgot about Cole.

Almost.

"Do you like this guy?"

I shrug.

"Were you guys serious?"

"Not really. I mean, we hooked up a few times at the club and then when I realized he was my professor—"

"What?" She jumps up. "Your professor?"

Laughing, I admit, "Yeah, I enrolled in an intro to law class, and he was my professor."

"Shut the fuck up."

"Right? I was all excited when I realized it, but then we got to know each other, and one thing led to another..." I don't complete that sentence. No need to. "He asked me to quit going to the club to exclusively date him."

"And you said yes?"

"I wasn't exactly sure. I haven't dated anyone since Carter. I was willing to give it a try, but the next day everything blew up, and I realized it was Carter, and here we are."

"So...have you talked to this guy?"

"No."

"But he's Carter's friend?"

"I guess. We haven't talked about it, but I know they know each other."

I take a deep breath, standing up before I say, "I've got to go pack. Carter's going to be here pretty soon, and I have to shower and get ready first."

Kaitlyn nods, and I walk down the hallway with a mess of thoughts running through my head. After jumping in the shower, I let the hot water pound down on my chest before I walk my head under the stream, letting it fall down my face, and hide the tears that instantly start to fall.

———————————

Saying goodbye to Kaitlyn was harder than I thought it would be, but I promised her I'd keep in touch, and we even planned a trip for her to come visit me in San Francisco.

Carter and I were able to switch seats with other passengers so we could sit together. We were both exhausted from our night of talking so, thankfully, I was able to lift my armrest and curl up next to him to sleep the entire flight home. Being back in his arms felt so real. So right. Like the past ten years hadn't happened, and we are the same two people.

"So you'll come to the drive tomorrow?" Carter asks, standing at my doorway after he walked me to my place.

"Of course. Do I get to meet the little guy too?"

Carter laughs to himself. "He'd like that."

"He would?" I ask, a little confused.

"Yeah. He knows all about you."

"He does?"

"Let's just say he's given me advice a time or two."

"How old is he?" I ask in disbelief.

He shakes his head. "Never mind." He leans in to kiss my lips softly. "I'll see you tomorrow."

"Tomorrow…" I whisper as he walks away, and I shut the door.

Chapter 33

EVANGELINE

My stomach turns when I see the banner for the event saying it's hosted by none other than Cole's law firm.

I look around and see Cole on one side of the event and Carter on the other. Seemingly they look to be in their own separate worlds, but I can tell their tension is so thick you could cut it with a knife.

Carter and I never discussed the club or Cole while in Minnesota. I still don't know their story or how close they are, but something tells me that since he's involved in this event, there's more than just the club friendship there.

Well, at least there was more than the club.

They both look up and see me standing there, not sure which direction to move. After glancing at each other, then back to me, they both start in my direction.

Questions run through my mind. I did start to like Cole, and it was nice seeing Carter again, but are we still the same people? Have we grown so much that we won't like each other when real life kicks in? I know that Cole's personality fit pretty well with mine, but Carter and I fell right back into our friendship like no time had passed at all.

When Cole reaches me first, my head is spinning, and I hold up my hands. "Stop," I say, making sure he keeps his distance in front of Carter. I don't want to cause a scene at something that should be a promising event.

"I just want to make sure you're okay?" Cole asks, standing a few feet from me.

I take a weary breath. "I'm sorry I haven't returned any of your calls. I'm fine. You were right. I had to deal with my issues."

"Where were you?"

"She went home, with me," Carter says, stepping up right then, wrapping his arm around my shoulders and pumping out his chest like a lion staking his claim.

I look at him, not hiding my irritation and stepping out of his grip. "I didn't go *with* you. But yes, I went back to our hometown."

"Can we talk?" Cole asks, holding out his hand to me, and I look at it, then at Carter.

"Not here. This is all too much right now. I'm here to get tested for the little boy."

"It's this way," Carter says, placing his hand behind my back again to lead me away.

I catch him glaring at Cole, and I respond with pushing his arms off me. I may not know what's going on with either of them, but I won't have one staking claim on me like I'm a prize to be won. Even if it is Carter.

The test is a simple mouth swab, so it doesn't take long until I'm ready to leave and get away from the watchful eyes of two guys who I know are staring at my every move.

If only it were that easy.

I look over at Cole, who's waiting for me from where he was signing people into the drive. After taking a deep breath, I walk toward him. I can't be a bitch and ignore him just because it makes my life easier.

He walks away from the table and meets me halfway. "Did you really see him back home?"

I nod. "You have to understand. We have a lot of history together. History that was left unresolved."

"So where does that leave us?"

I look up at him, biting the inside of my cheek. His eyes are sad behind his glasses, and I can tell he's been running his hands through his hair by the extra messy look he's sporting now. "I honestly don't know."

"Do you still love him?"

"Cole, you can't ask me that. It's been years. But yes, at one point in my past I did. Very much."

He takes a deep breath, looking around the event while he tries to figure out what to say next.

"Do I even have a chance against him?" he asks flat-out.

"Yes. No. God. A girl needs to think, okay? Everything has happened so fast. Can we all pause so I can take in the fact that someone I haven't seen in ten years appeared out of the blue? I know this may suck for you, but please try to remember how I feel."

He steps up, grabbing my hand, trying to calm my sudden irritation. "Hey, I'm sorry. I get it. You take all the time you need. I'd like to see you if I can, though."

"We'll see, okay? Either way, I'll be in class on Monday. Maybe we can talk then."

He nods, giving my hand a tight squeeze, kissing my cheek before turning to walk away.

Carter quickly approaches me. "I'm sorry if I upset you earlier," he says as he holds out his hand low to grab ahold of mine.

"I'm sorry, too. I was caught off guard. I had no clue Cole would be here. So you guys are friends?"

"We were friends," he spits out.

"Carter…that's not fair. I don't want to come between you guys."

"You didn't. I swear. He's known for years how hard I've looked for you and how much of a mess I was without you. I don't know how he realized it was you, but any friend of mine would have told me right away, not try to make it so I never knew you were here."

I let out a deep sigh while rubbing my hands through my hair, frustrated with the entire situation.

When my bracelet runs down my arm, the sight of my tattoo catches my attention. I briefly close my eyes, turning my wrist out to display it for Carter. Our eyes meet, and he quickly holds his up to show the unchanged line we got ten years ago.

"That's how he knew." He pauses, looking around the event. "Do you like him?" Carter asks from out of nowhere.

I shrug. "I don't know."

"Were you really going to date him like he said you guys were?"

I shrug. "I was."

"Was…? So not anymore?"

"No. Yes. Shit, I don't know. I told him the same thing. Everything just happened so fast."

"But what about us? Evangeline, I've never stopped looking for you, and I never stopped loving you."

"That was a long time ago, Carter. What if who we were back then isn't who we are now? All we have is the past. Is that enough for us to hold a future?"

"You know it is. We knew it back then. What we had was something special."

I sigh. He's right. It really was. And I'd be lying if I said I didn't think about him every day for all these years.

"It's going to take time," I admit. "We can't just pick up where we left off. I need to figure things out first."

"I've got all the time in the world. I've waited this long having no clue where you were. I'm not going to let you go again."

I look into his eyes, seeing every ounce of determination he put into that statement. It's the same look I've dreamed about for years. The look he gave me when he left for college. He said we'd be together forever and that he'd come get me from our hometown as soon as he could. I believed him then just as I do now.

"Come on," he says, grabbing my hand and pulling me away from the crowd. "I want to introduce you to Kyle."

I follow him into the hospital, and we enter a room where a young boy is sitting up in his bed playing on his phone.

"You better not be practicing our racing game on the app," Carter announces as he enters the room.

The kid drops the phone instantly, hiding it under his blanket. "What, you scared?" he teases back.

Carter reaches for the phone, turning it to reveal the game he was talking about. "Yeah, I see how you cheat."

"It's not cheating, it's practice. Practice makes perfect, remember?"

"Okay, smart-ass," Carter says, engulfing the boy in his arms and rubbing his head with a closed fist.

The boy laughs while trying to stop the attack and when Carter finally lets him sit back, he hits his shoulder, saying, "Guess who this is?"

"Shut up! You mean you actually do have a life outside of here?" he teases.

"Yes, I do…" he deadpans.

"Don't lie," I jump in on the conversation. "I can only imagine how he throws his life into the hospital. I bet he's here even on his days off, huh?"

"Dude! All the time. You'd think he was the sick person in this situation."

"What? Is it a crime that I like to hang out with you?"

He looks at him like he's crazy. "I'm eleven. You're how old? Yes, I'd say it's a crime that hanging out with me is more fun than your real life."

"Don't worry. He was the same back in high school. It took years for him to actually notice me and ask me out," I tease, winking at Carter.

"Okay, that's enough of bash on Carter time. Kyle, I'd like for you to meet Evangeline."

I reach out my hand to shake his, and instead, he gives me a fist bump, and after we hit, he blows it up.

"I taught him that," Carter brags.

I can't help but smile at the man, and the doctor Carter has become. If his other patients are anything like Kyle, Carter has left quite the impression on these young kids just like he did on me so many years ago. I'd be lying if I said those feelings from the past don't come creeping back in.

"Dr. Donovan," a nurse calls from the door. "You're needed in the tent."

"I'll be right there," he responds. "Okay, man, now you've met her, you know I'm not lying, so there. Now I have to get back to, I don't know, saving lives, possibly yours," he boasts out.

"Was his ego always this big?" Kyle asks, looking at me.

"No, I think that's something he's earned over the years," I answer.

Carter grins at me then we say our goodbyes and walk back to the tent.

"He's a pretty cool kid," I say.

"Yeah. Let's hope we can find him a donor today."

"We will. I feel it."

He leans down to give me a hug goodbye. For the first time, I almost panic. I'm not ready to say goodbye, so I blurt out, "Want to read those letters tonight?"

He leans in, whispering, "Hell yes, I do. I'll be over at seven. Sounds good? I'll bring food."

I let out a sigh of relief. "Sounds good."

Chapter 34

EVANGELINE

I have to catch my breath for a second after I open the door. I'm still shocked that this is Carter, and he's here in my place. After years of yearning for him and also trying to forget about him, everything still seems so surreal.

We stare at each other for a little longer than we should, and when his lips curl up into a small smile, I pull the door open further, silently inviting him into my home for the first time. He leans in to kiss my cheek hello then sets the Mexican food he brought down on my counter.

"I hope you like burritos. There's a killer place on 24th and Mission, so I stopped by real quick before coming here, with no sour cream, of course." He winks, and I love that he remembers my distaste for sour cream.

It's so stupid that something so small could mean so much, but it does. Maybe we haven't changed as much as I thought.

I grab two plates out of the cupboard along with some forks and knives when the size of these things catches my attention. "There's no way I can eat all of that," I exclaim as I motion to the monstrosity he just set on my plate.

"Then good, you'll have leftovers for tomorrow. Where should we sit?"

I motion to the nook that holds a tiny table for two. I live in a small studio apartment in the Mission District. The place is only a few hundred square feet, but the rent is cheap, and the neighborhood is full of people my age, so it's been perfect.

"Let me get the box of letters," I say as I start to walk to my closet, but he stops me.

"We can eat first. There's no rush. We've waited for ten years. We can wait for a few more minutes. I want to hear more about you. What have you been up to these last ten years? I hear you work for a law firm."

"How did you know that?"

He looks my way, and I stop short. Cole. Right, of course, he knew that from him. I shake my head. I don't want to go there right now, so I continue like that moment didn't just happen.

"Yes, I'm a legal assistant for this amazing attorney who has taught me so much that I've really grown to love the legal system. That's why I enrolled in the Intro to Law class. I'm thinking of going back to school, but wanted to make sure I was up for it before I jumped in feet first."

"I'll have to admit, the girl who wanted to break the law at any opportunity she could becoming a lawyer makes me laugh, but honestly, I think you'd be really good at it. You always knew how to outrun the law, so I can see you being able to solve it just the same."

I laugh out loud because he's so right. It does take a criminal mind to be able to solve a crime, and though I never got arrested or anything, I was able to have my share of fun and never got caught.

"I've really enjoyed the class so far, and if I can pull it off, I'm going to enroll and start working my way toward my degree."

"I would say with your background of already working at a firm you'd have a head start on the system and how it works."

"Yeah, that's what I was thinking. You can read all you want but nothing compares to real life experience and that I have plenty of. Plus, my boss, Kamii, is so supportive, and I know she'll help me at every step."

"Man, Evangeline." He shakes his head, raising his eyebrows slightly. "I'm so proud to see what you've become. I've been afraid all this time that you were alone, barely making ends meet and here, this whole time, you've been kicking ass and taking names. I'm really impressed."

"That means a lot to me to hear you say. I was lost for a few years but something led me to the firm, and things took off from there. Everything happens for a reason, right?"

He smiles, slowly nodding his head. "Right."

Carter inhales his entire burrito as I can barely finish a third of mine. We crack up at old memories and even about stories we've experienced while apart. Our friendship is like we haven't skipped a day, and a small part of me is hoping this is the beginning to us again.

After we wash our dishes, we both grab a beer from the fridge and head to the couch to finally open a box that has haunted me for years. With my hands hovering over the lid, I look at him for his final approval before I lift it, knowing we can never go back.

He doesn't nod or even smile. Instead, he puts down his beer, stands up to where I am, kissing me on my head, and places his hands over mine, so we lift the lid together.

I blink away the tears that fill my eyes when I see the letters I've seen for the last ten years that have piled up. On every envelope, up in the corner is their address in Sonoma.

When Carter sees the address, he turns to me. "They live that close?"

I let out a much-needed laugh of relief. "Yes. I had him here in San Francisco. I chose them because they owned a winery, and I knew they'd be able to give him a life you and I only dreamed of having."

Our eyes meet, and I can see his understanding in my thinking, which makes me hopeful.

"Should we start at the top or go by the dates and start at the beginning?" I ask, pulling all the letters out of the box.

"I can't believe there are so many," he states in mild shock at the pile.

"They've written me a couple times a year since he was born. She knew I was having a very difficult time with my decision and promised, mom to mom, that she'd give our son the best life possible, and she'd document it every step of the way for me. I couldn't open them when they came, but every time one arrived, a sense of relief would flood me, and I knew he was doing well. That's all I needed to know then."

"I'm glad you waited for me."

A tear slips from my eye. "Me too."

He leans over to wipe my cheek before looking back at the pile. "Let's start from the beginning." He smiles as his eyes light up. "Let's watch him grow up."

My heart hurts from the thought. It breaks knowing I've missed so much, but I feel it slowly repairing with every breath I take sitting here with Carter.

The first letter comes a month after he was born, and it's here that he learns his full name, Benjamin Carter Adams.

"His middle name is Carter?" He looks at me in shock.

"They wanted him to have something tied to me in terms of his name, so I asked them to choose Carter as his middle name," I say, not stopping the tears this time.

He grabs the letter and folds it open to reveal a picture of a baby boy dressed in a San Francisco Giants onesie that says Future MVP. Carter's head falls back on the couch, and even though his eyes are closed, the wetness seeping out makes my tears fall even more.

"That's our baby, Carter. We made him."

He opens his eyes, letting the tears fall down his cheeks. "I can't believe it. That's our son."

I lean back, cuddling in his arms as he holds up the picture for us both to look at. "It is. Our miracle."

I grab the next one. "Look, he's sitting up and eating baby food in this photo."

We both laugh at the happy boy with green mush smeared all over his face.

When we opened the letter that showed him taking his first steps we both cried happy tears, admiring the photo of Benjamin running toward his father. The look on his dad's face heals the wounds I never thought would be mended. In every photo his adoptive parents are in, they look incredibly happy holding the gift of life that we were able to give them. The thought makes my heart sing.

We spend the night going through each letter, both of us crying at times and other times smiling from ear to ear as we hear his accomplishments. We've learned he's a straight A student, which he obliviously got from Carter, and he likes to stir up trouble from time to time, which no doubt he got from me. He's a perfect blend of us in personality and looks, and at the end of the night, I couldn't be more proud of the young man he's become.

As we fold the last letter back into the envelope, a nervousness creeps over my skin as I wonder what happens next.

Thankfully, Carter takes charge, pulling me into his arms, not saying a word but taking the photos we set off to the side and flipping through them one more time.

We laugh at certain ones and even point out things we didn't notice the first time.

There's no rush. We sit staring at photos, holding each other like we have all the time in the world.

Once we get to the last photo again, he puts the stack down beside him, resting his head against mine as we lean back on the couch.

After taking a deep breath, he says, "Well, it's late, so I guess I'll head out."

He stands up, and I follow his lead.

"Oh, it's okay. Um, I mean—"

"Hey." He turns to me, placing his hand on the back of my neck and wrapping his fingers through my hair. "I don't want you to feel pressured having me here and worried about what happens next. We have time. It's been a big night. I'll see you tomorrow?"

Hearing how supportive he's being of me makes me want him to stay, but I know he's right. We've had a crazy emotional night, and we shouldn't confuse our feelings with what we just shared and what we are doing with us.

One thing at a time.

I lean up to kiss his cheek. "Thank you, Carter."

He holds my head in both his hands, looking into my eyes. "That doesn't mean I'm not going to kiss you." He smirks as his lips reach mine.

His kiss is soft, seductive, and mind-blowing. The way his tongue softly sweeps over mine, taking my breath completely away, almost brings me to my knees. To my dismay, he keeps it short, pulling back and kissing my forehead before turning toward the door.

"Thank you for sharing those with me. It"—he pauses for a moment—"it really means a lot."

He opens the door, and I hold it halfway open, leaning my body against it. "Me too."

Something red catches my eyes, and I look down at the floor to see a dozen roses, wrapped tightly in plastic wrap. I look at Carter in question, but he shakes his head. Both of us realize at the same time who they must have come from.

Cole.

Chapter 35

COLE

The flowers I brought to surprise Evangeline with mocked me while they sat on the floor next to her door. I saw Carter walking into her complex when I turned the corner and against my better judgment, I still went to her place to torture myself. I never knocked or let them know I was there, but I sat with my ear close to her door for a half hour and heard more than I ever wanted to hear.

I'm fucked. How can I compete with what they have? I couldn't hear every word, but even I could tell their relationship has picked up exactly where it left off. When they started opening letters about their son I had to leave. I couldn't take it anymore.

Now I sit here like a little bitch biting my nails in anticipation for her to walk through the door. I'm not the guy who worries about girls or even chases after them.

Class starts at six and here it is, six-oh-two, and she's still not here. The feelings running through me are exactly why I don't date.

This sucks to no end.

Pissed at myself for feeling this way, I shake my head and stand up, ready to start the lecture. I write something on the board, and when I turn around, I see her, standing at the door. She looks just as timid as I feel. The look on her face isn't promising, so I try to put on my game face and announce, "I'm glad you could join us tonight, Evangeline," but instantly regret the ticked off tone it comes out as.

She slowly takes her seat, and I start the next few painful hours that I hope will fly by. I used to love seeing her sitting front row but not tonight. I try to keep my head up and my professionalism on point, but nothing seems to be working. My gaze always goes right to her.

I write notes on the board, and when I turn around, I notice Charlie has moved a few seats and is leaning over, whispering something to Evangeline. Instantly my blood starts to boil, and when Charlie looks up, his eyes meet mine, and I swear the prick challenges me.

I look at Evangeline, and by the way her eyes won't look my way I know whatever just happened, it has to do with her and me.

Thankfully she stays after class and slowly makes her way to my desk.

"What did Charlie say to you in class?"

She bites her bottom lip. "He asked if we had a lovers' quarrel."

My head drops to my chest, ashamed. "Fuck, was I that obvious?"

She doesn't respond, which kills me even more. I stand up from my seat and walk to the opposite side of my desk to be closer to her.

Grabbing her hand, I ask, "Have you had dinner yet?"

She nods.

"Want a ride home then?"

"Yeah, that'd be nice."

We walk to the car, and on the way home it's quiet with anticipation that's killing me.

"So, how was your trip home?" I finally say, trying to break the ice.

"It was really good actually. I got to see my friend that I haven't seen or talked to in ten years. The town hasn't changed much, but it was nice to see—"

"Carter," I interrupt, kicking myself the minute the words left my mouth. *How could I be so stupid?*

"That's not what I was going to say, but yeah, he showed up the last day I was there."

"And…?"

"And what, Cole?" She shrugs.

I sigh, ready to ask more questions but when I park and look up, Carter is standing outside her complex, waiting for her to come home.

"Looks like you have company," I say, nodding my head to her door.

I meet eyes with Carter and watch as his hands ball into fists at his side. As we exit the car, he storms toward us with an authority I've never seen him display.

Even though Carter is bigger than me, I'm ready to stand my ground and not back down if he wants to actually go to blows over this entire situation. Shit, it will probably help my built up frustrations.

Evangeline is quick to get in between us, putting her hand up to Carter as he approaches. "He was just giving me a ride home from school."

"Yeah, I'm sure that's not all he hoped you'd ride," Carter spits out, glaring at me.

"Real nice, Carter," Evangeline says, shaking her head.

Even I'm shocked he'd say something so vulgar to Evangeline, and I love to know I'm getting under his skin so much that he's not thinking straight.

"Fuck, I didn't mean it like that," Carter says, grabbing her hand.

"Don't forget he's the one who knew it was you the entire time at the club. Why do you think he was so *secretive*?"

Carter gasps and stares at me. I smirk, glad I hit a nerve. Obviously, that hasn't been brought up between the two of them.

"He's the one who tried to kick me out of the club so you'd never know it was me," Carter fights back.

"You know what, you're right. Screw both of you guys. You can have your pissing contest alone, without me here," she states, turning to walk down the hallway to her place.

I glare at Carter. "Real nice, asshole."

He turns to follow her, and even though I don't want to, I walk back to my car. Since I know I was dealt the short stick here, I'll do anything I need to do to make sure I stay on Evangeline's good side while I still have a fighting chance.

Evangeline

"Just go away, Carter," I state as we walk down the hall.

"Let me explain."

I turn to face him. "Explain what? That you knew it was me the entire time? That you let me have sex with you knowing I didn't know it was you." I push at his chest.

He stands still, not saying a word.

"I'm sorry, Evangeline. I didn't know what to do. I was in shock. Here I've looked for you for ten years and then you show up out of the blue. What was I to do?"

"Hmm, well, gee, how about tell me who the fuck you are?" I yell.

I can't believe I was so caught up in seeing him again and didn't think that I should still be mad at him for this.

Quietly he says, "I was afraid you'd run again," while reaching out to hold my hand, looking down at the way they interconnect. "You don't understand. I had to play it cool. I found you, and I was terrified to lose you again." His head tilts up, and our eyes meet. "I wanted to see if our connection was still there. I wanted to know if you could feel me the way I felt you."

I turn in the hallway to lean on the wall and rest my head against it, taking in a deep breath.

He steps closely in front of me, placing his feet on either side of mine. His warmth overwhelms my senses, and suddenly, I don't remember why I was mad at him.

"You did too. You realized it was me without me having to say anything. That's how strong this is."

His hand reaches up and moves my hair out of my face, tucking it behind my ear.

My lips tremble with want and fear. Everything he said is true. When he kissed me that first time, I was gone. Even then my body knew it was him, my brain just hadn't caught up yet.

When his lips lightly brush against mine the thought angers me again, and I push him away, walking into my apartment and closing the door behind me. Leaving him alone in the hallway.

I hear him slam his fist against the wall, and all I can do is pray he didn't leave a mark for me to be reminded of him every day.

Chapter 36

COLE

It's been a week now, and I'm nowhere close to where I want to be. Evangeline has been coming to class, and we've talked but nothing more. I'm kicking myself for canceling my membership to Bridge, and you can bet yourself that I sat outside, so thankful when she never showed up last night.

I don't know why, though. There's nothing I could have done, and it would have killed me knowing she was in someone else's arms with me sitting right outside. Maybe I like self-torture because I seem to be putting myself through it a lot lately.

Tonight I'm finally getting my chance to make my case. I know he has her past, but I need to remind her that she left him for a reason.

Saturday night can be crazy everywhere you go. I was reminded of our time at the taco truck, and I knew where to take her. It was so simple, yet that's when I felt we were really us for the first time.

She's a small town girl, and I can tell she's more comfortable at a hole-in-the-wall place rather than a five-star restaurant.

We cross the Golden Gate and pull off the freeway in Larkspur to a small place I know on the water.

Her knee bounces slightly next to me, and I'm sad to see her nerves on display. She's never been this way before when we were together.

I place my hand on her, steadying her movements. "Nothing's different here. It's still me."

Our eyes meet, and I see the slight smile I was hoping for. She nods then opens the door after I put the car in park.

I reach for her hand and love that she holds mine like she wants to, not like she feels she has to.

We sit, order our drinks, and I lean back in my chair, smiling at the way her face is lit up by the light shining around her like she's the angel I've dreamed of.

"Tell me about your week?" I ask, hoping to start a normal conversation to prove this is still us and nothing has changed.

She shrugs. "Pretty uneventful. How about you?"

"I'm working on a crazy case right now that's nowhere near as fun as my last one where I got to spend all day getting to know this amazing woman."

She rolls her eyes and laughs at my comment. "Sorry, not all of your co-workers can be so amazing."

"Ain't that the truth? Now I'm working with Karl, and he smells nowhere near as good as you."

She smirks and picks up her menu, obviously done with that part of our conversation.

The rest of our night pretty much goes the same way. Something's different. She's different.

The easiness of our relationship before just flowed, and now I feel like I'm pulling teeth to get the girl I knew back. She's being friendly, and our conversation is there but not like it was.

I appreciate that she's trying, and I can tell she is, but God I want her to try harder.

What else can I do to show her I'm the one, not him?

A fear I've never felt starts to take me over when thoughts of her going back to him enter my mind.

If we're having trouble connecting the same way as before in conversation, then I need an opportunity to show her how we were sexually. The last time I was with her, in my bed, it was magical.

That's what we need again. Then she'll see that what we were starting was something special.

The rain has lightly started to come down, so we run to the car after dinner and head back to her place. I definitely haven't gotten the vibe that the date is coming to an end, and I pray she gives me a shot to prove to her once more who we are when we're together.

I park and turn her way, waiting, praying, for an invite inside. When she smiles, my heart melts, and I know I'm in.

"Would you like to come inside?" she asks, tilting her head slightly toward her place.

"You know I would. Wait, stay there." I wink and open the door to my car.

It's pouring rain, so I grab my jacket and go to her side, holding it over us as we run to her place.

What I didn't expect was to see a man, a man I know all too well, sitting on the doorstep of her place, soaking wet.

He glares in our direction and instantly Evangeline steps out of my makeshift umbrella, standing in the rain rather than be seen next to me. She looks at Carter, then back at me, and that's it.

That look right there said it all. She was more worried about Carter's reaction than mine. Her mind might not know what she wants, but her instincts just decided for her, and it's not me.

Instead of backing away like I should, knowing I'm not the one, anger builds inside me at him. This is all his fault. I was almost there. She was letting me in. If I had been able to show her what we were, she would have been mine forever.

Carter must feel the same rage I do because within seconds of us arriving, he's up on his feet, coming right for me.

"Cole, you need to back the fuck off," he bites out while pushing me back.

Carter's bigger than me and his sudden assault caught me off guard. I've known the guy for a few years now, and I've never seen him show the smallest bit of anger toward anyone, well, anyone but her.

I smile at the thought. "Nope, sorry." I don't push him back but stand eye-to-eye with him. "She already told you ten years ago when she left you and gave up your child without even a mention of his existence to you. Remember?"

I stare into his eyes, daring him to take it further, so I'm not the first one to swing on someone who used to be my best friend.

"What the fuck did you just say?" He steps up closer, pushing me with his chest.

"You guys, stop," Evangeline yells, but both of us only see or hear rage.

"You heard me. I was there for every pathetic moment. You had your chance, now back off, she's mine."

The rain running down my glasses blocks my vision, and the slamming of his fist against my jaw takes me by surprise. I fall back but jump up quickly and run toward him, cutting down low to try to bring him to the ground.

He loses his balance, and we both tumble to the ground. I get in one hit to his stomach, but within seconds, he's got me in a headlock, and I reach up, tearing at his shirt, desperately trying for any leverage.

The rain has us sliding around, making it hard for me to get my footing, and it's not until I feel Evangeline kicking both of us, demanding for us to stop that I realize what exactly just went down.

Carter lets go, and we both push back on the ground, breathing hard and glaring at each other.

"Have you two lost your minds?" Evangeline yells.

I watch as Carter snaps out of his anger fueled rage and goes to stand up, but she stops him. "Don't you dare," she demands. "I can't believe you two. You can't fight for me like I'm a prize to be won."

She turns to walk into her place, and I watch as Carter sits on his knees, slamming his hands to the ground and yelling out in frustration.

He knows he fucked up with her this time and a sense of satisfaction runs through me. If I'm not the one she wants, I'm happy knowing now maybe he won't have a chance with her either.

Chapter 37

EVANGELINE

My phone dings with a text message from Carter.

Please talk to me.

Why, Carter? I told you, we can't just pick up where we left off. There's just too much history between us.

Do you remember the time we spent down at the lake when I got my acceptance letter?

I sigh, dropping my head back against my couch. How could I forget? Our whole relationship started with that one night.

Of course I do.

That's why. I loved you even before that night. And when you found out I was leaving you were scared. I saw it in your eyes. I see that same fear every time I see you now.

I close my eyes, fighting the burn of the tears that want to come alive.

It's been ten years, yet nothing has changed.

Yes, it has. Everything has changed.

No, Evangeline. Nothing has. You knew it when I kissed you. Please don't fight it anymore. Please don't punish me for going away.

I'm not punishing you.

I promised you I'd come back for you, and we'd stand at the starting line together. I've kept my promise.

He sends me a picture that nearly rips me in two. I had joked around our last night before he left saying once we were able to get back together we should add to our tattoos. At that point, we could turn our starting line into an infinity sign with the line running through it, to prove our line is as thick as steel and nothing could ever break it.

He got the tattoo.

I sit in silence, staring at the picture. I can't believe he remembered.

Can I please come over? I'll make you an early dinner.

Okay.

Is all I responded after a few minutes. I couldn't think of what else to say. Biting my inner lip, I stare out the window of my place. Maybe it's time to finally open that side of me again.

COLE

After spending all day Sunday sulking by myself, I finally got shit-faced drunk until I passed out on my couch.

She hasn't answered any of my calls, and today is a holiday, so our class is canceled. Saturday night was bad, but I thought I'd give it one more shot to see if I have any chance of winning her affection.

I'm sure her work is closed too, so I took a chance and headed to her place, hoping I could surprise her and take her out for dinner. What I didn't plan on was Carter beating me to the punchline.

I didn't see his car, but after knocking on her door, she answered only for me to see Carter standing right there in her kitchen. I look around the room and by the empty plates on her table and the sink full of dishes I can tell he's been here awhile.

"Hey," I say to her.

"Hi," she responds, glancing back at Carter before me.

I hate to see the two sets of eyes both searching mine for an answer. Carter sets the towel down he was holding, and Evangeline takes a deep breath in, gripping the door like she's waiting to slam it shut if things arise.

And yes, she would slam it shut on me in a heartbeat. I can see it in her eyes.

They want to know why I'm here and I stand, helpless, doing nothing but wracking my brain for what to say.

Time ticks by and finally Carter breaks the silence, "Listen, Cole—"

I hold up my hand, stopping him mid-sentence.

Evangeline slips in between the two of us, protecting who, though, I don't know.

"Not here, you guys. We're not doing this again," she says, with her back to me. "Cole." She turns, placing her hand on my chest and with the slightest of ease, pushes me back, away from her door.

"Wait," I demand, standing my ground.

Carter glares at me while Evangeline takes a gasp of breath in, shaking her head almost in disbelief. Her eyes tell no lie. She wants him, and he's officially won her back.

The realization finally hits me. I don't have any place here. For years I've listened to Carter whine about how much he needed this girl in his life. I, of all people, shouldn't be the one trying to prevent them from finally being together.

It's time. There's nothing more I can do but throw in the towel. He's won, and now I must be the man I wish to be and respectfully bow out while I can still hold my head high.

"Can we talk? Both of you?" I ask, looking at Carter.

After glancing at each other, they both shrug but keep silent.

"God, this sucks," I say, rubbing the back of my neck before taking a deep breath. Being the bigger man is much harder than I ever thought it would be. I sigh, shaking my head before looking back up. "Fuck it. I've been thinking a lot, and I know what the right thing to do here is."

Evangeline and Carter both look at each other again in question.

"Evangeline," I say, staring directly into her eyes and reaching out to hold her fingers, trying to show her I'm tip-toeing around here and not trying to overtake the situation. Thankfully she understands my gesture and allows me to hold her this way.

"You're something special, you know that?"

She nervously bites her inner lip but doesn't pull her hand away.

"I should have known it was you after all I've heard these past years because I fell for you just the way this shmuck did."

I hear Carter huff, but I try to continue, having to clear the pain from my throat I felt sneak its way up when I admit I fell for her.

"I can't compete here. You two have more history and unfinished business than I'll ever be able to stand up to. So even though my heart breaks to do this"—I pause, clearing my throat again and looking away for a brief moment—"it will break more when you give me a chance only to realize later that he's the one you're meant to be with."

"Cole." Evangeline squeezes my hand, holding on to more than just my fingers.

"I won't be the one to come between love. What you guys have is something people dream about and to find each other again, the way you did…" I shake my head in disbelief. "That's fate and who am I to come between fate. So, Carter, you better be the man she deserves and don't fuck it up this time."

He smirks as he looks over at Evangeline. "You know I won't."

"Yes, unfortunately, I do." I turn my attention back to her. "Honestly, I should hate you for all you put him through and how I had to listen to him bitch for so many years," I taunt, trying to break the pain in my heart with humor. "But seriously, I wish you both the best."

With that, I lean over to Evangeline, kiss her on her cheek, and Carter comes closer as he reaches out to shake my hand. He mouths *thank you* to me, and I nod before walking away.

Chapter 38

EVANGELINE

I close the door behind Cole and look at Carter in question. He's been here for about an hour, and things have been good. Friendly, comfortable even. We haven't talked about anything pertaining to us, but after that speech, I know our time has come.

Slowly he walks toward me, entangling my hands in his.

"So you'd bitch about me?" I ask with a small smile shining through.

He tilts his head to the side. "Not *all* the time," he teases.

"But you really looked for me? For all those years?"

"I never stopped looking. I knew I'd find you one day."

"So now that you found me, what do you plan to do?"

"Never let you out of my sight again." He leans in, holding me tightly and kissing my lips like he should have been every day for the last ten years.

My hands reach up, wrapping around his neck, and I pull him down closer to me, not letting him back away this time. I want this. I want him.

He gets my drift, and in one swift movement, he picks me up and walks me over to my bed. I make him laugh when he tries to put me down, but my grip is so tight he can't position us correctly without falling on his hands.

I don't care, though. I wasn't sure what I was going to do until I saw Cole standing at my door. My first thought was *no, please don't make Carter think we're still together,* and suddenly, it was clear as day. Any question I had was completely erased from my mind and only being with him filled every thought.

Now I want to feel him, knowing for the first time that it's truly him, on every millimeter covering my entire body.

He takes my hands, releasing my grip from his neck and holding them above my head when he whispers, "You don't need to hold me down this time. I wouldn't leave even if you tried to kick me out. You're stuck with me. I hope you know that." His lips brush mine before moving on to my neck.

Dropping my head back, I push my chest out to him, knowing he'll do exactly what I want to my breasts and nothing that I don't.

I feel his fingers unbuttoning my blouse, and the cool breeze that washes over me is brief until his warmth wraps around me, holding my body tight while he worships his way down my chest, onto my stomach and back up.

After removing my shirt and bra, he sits back on his heels, taking off his own shirt, and for the first time I truly get to admire the man he's become. I lift up, wanting to run my fingers over his body, but he stops me short and grabs my wrist. Pushing the bracelet I'm wearing down and matching our tattoos together.

"Here we are, at the starting line. It's not a race, but rather a marathon, and I'm going to love you till the very end. I promise you that," he says before he kisses my wrist, wrapping it around his neck and bringing my bare breasts to his.

My heart pounds out of my chest as I'm overtaken by a wave of emotions I can barely handle. He encloses me in his arms, holding me tightly until I can take a deep, calming breath. Slowly, he lowers me back down. I close my eyes, still trying to calm my breath when his hands start to unbutton my pants and slip them down my legs.

Surprise makes me squeal when his warm tongue licks me before I feel him anywhere else. I open my eyes and lift my body up to my elbows, only to see the sexiest smirk I've ever seen, looking that much better in between my legs.

I can't help the laugh that comes out of my mouth before his hands push me back down, spreading my legs wide, giving him full access.

The way his tongue works my clit while his fingers curl inside me makes my body start to quiver with a building need to search for its release. My hands wrap around his head, pulling him in closer as I unapologetically start to ride his face.

A deep desire I've never felt overwhelms me, causing me to barely catch my breath, but to my dismay, Carter stops, flipping me to my side before he removes his own pants.

"No," I whine out, feeling like I'm going to die if I don't explode first.

He laughs before lying down behind me, pulling his naked body flush with mine. His cock pushes between my legs, rubbing my clit but not coming anywhere near my entrance, rather rubbing right over it.

Pushing himself against me and away makes me slam the bed next to me, dying that much more to have him inside me.

"Carter," I yell.

Still on my side, his large hand grips the side of my ass cheek, and he lifts it, just enough to cause my entrance to open slightly before closing it again. I've never been so aware of that exact spot on my body and how extremely empty it is right now.

Two, three, four times he pulls my ass cheek up and then pushes it back down while alternately rubbing his cock in between my legs. He's so close, and I've never wanted someone to fuck me this badly, and knowing it's Carter makes my heart feel like it's going to burst right here.

"Please," I beg.

His lips come close to me from behind, and his warm breath tickles me, sending chills down my spine. Kissing the spot right behind my ear, I hear him whisper, "What, Evangeline? What do you want?"

"I want you. Please," I barely get out as he lifts my ass one more time.

"You promise?"

My brain isn't functioning. I can't think straight, and my head drops back to his in frustration.

"Please, Carter, please fuck me now."

He lifts my ass one more time, this time, positioning himself right where I want him, instantly warming the spot that was cold with every cool breeze he'd allow in. He doesn't push inside, though.

I want to growl at him, but I'm panting so hard I can't form the words.

"You're mine, Evangeline. This." He slides inside me, and the sensation that flies through my body creates a moan I've never heard from my mouth. "You. Me." He pulls all the way out, and I slam my hand against the bed in protest. He slides back in as he wraps his arm around me, pulling me tightly into his chest and running his hand up my neck, holding the back of my head against his face. "Are forever," he grunts out as he pumps inside me.

"Yes! Forever," I scream, letting him completely take over every aspect of my body, giving in fully to him, where I always should have been.

He pulls back out, but before I can yell at him for doing so, he moves me to my back, sliding on top of me, and kisses my lips as he slides in again, holding me tightly as he makes love to me all night long.

Chapter 39

CARTER

"Dr. Donovan, you have a call on line two," a nurse tells me as I walk down the hall.

"This is Dr. Donovan," I say after I pick up the receiver.

"You did it," I hear someone say, and before I can ask what they're talking about, they continue. "We found a match for your patient at the event you put together." I hear Kathy, the woman who helped me organize the donor drive.

"Yes!" I cheer. "So it's someone local then? Are they coming in?"

"Yes, they've already been contacted and have agreed to go through with the procedure. And guess what? The donor works at the law firm you got to sponsor the event, so I guess you deserve the credit for finding the donor, not us."

Nope. Not me. Cole.

Dammit. Is my first thought but then I shake my head. I shouldn't feel that way. This is for Kyle. We found him a donor, and right now, that's all that matters.

Kathy gives me the rest of the information and tells me when I should expect the donor to come in. We hang up, and I know there's one more thing I need to do before I go in search of Kyle and his parents.

I pick up my cell phone and press the name of someone I'd never thought I'd call again.

The phone rings, and just when I think it's going to voicemail, he picks up. "Please don't make me regret answering this phone call. You already got the girl. Don't rub it in."

"I'm not. I'm calling to tell you we found a donor for Kyle from the event. Turns out it's someone from your work."

"No shit?"

"Yeah. I can't tell you how happy I am right now." I guess I mean more than Kyle and his donor. I owe Cole for a lot of things. No matter what just happened, he was there for me for a long time, and now that I have Evangeline back, I can truly see I was able to make it through some really bad times because of him.

He pauses before responding, "I'm glad to hear it. Tell the little man to get better now, okay?"

"Okay."

We both sit on the line, not saying a word for a few breaths when I finally speak up. "Hey, Cole. I'm, I guess I'm calling to say thank you."

"Any time, bro," he says, putting my mind at ease. It may take time, but one day we could have some kind of friendship again.

We hang up, and I turn, ready to run down the hallway to tell Kyle and his parents the good news.

"Are we celebrating or what?" Evangeline says as she enters my place with a bottle of champagne.

We've been together every night since Cole left her place after he bowed out respectfully, finally showing me the man I know he really is. I can't blame the guy one bit, though. I've gone crazy over Evangeline too, so I know the blind haze he was under.

I pick her up, swinging her around, enjoying the absolute bliss my life has become in such a short amount of time. Finally having her back is a dream come true, and finding a donor for Kyle is my cherry on top.

"I still can't believe it," I admit. "I felt so helpless not being able to do anything and when I got the phone call today." I put her down, dropping my head back in relief. "Man, it was just the best feeling ever." I sigh with nothing but happiness creeping up my face.

"So how did you tell his parents?"

I laugh out loud. "You should have seen it. I ran to their room, literally falling over when I tripped on a chair that was sitting in his doorway. Of course Kyle gave me shit for it, but it was awesome to rile him right back by saying, 'I may be a klutz, but I'm finally going to save your ass.'"

I pause, having to take a breath before the emotions of telling them take over and tears of joy spill from my eyes. Evangeline notices my moment and wraps her arms around me, bringing her lips to mine.

"I love you, Dr. Carter Donovan," she says while dropping her head to my chest. "I still can't believe I'm here. With you. Who would have thought?"

We sit in an embrace for a moment. I question if I should bring it up but decide it's worth it.

"So I didn't tell you who the actual donor was."

"Yeah?"

"It was someone who works with Cole."

Her eyes get big. "Really?"

"Yeah, and, I, um, called him today," I stutter, hoping I'm making the right choice by bringing him up.

We haven't spoken about him, but I know she's seen him in class. I'll admit, I was a little nervous about her being there, but she assured me there was nothing to worry about, and after Cole's speech, I feel like I can trust him too.

"And…?" she asks suspiciously.

"And, I'm glad I did." I nod, feeling at peace with my decision to call him. She eyes me like she wants more information, so I continue, "It was short but, I don't know, nice, I guess. I thanked him and"—I shrug—"it was like old times for that brief moment."

She hugs me again. "I'm so glad to hear. It still breaks my heart that you guys aren't friends anymore."

I stay silent. For the first time I don't feel the anger that I've felt when his name comes up and any mention of our recent past. I do miss my friend and who knows, maybe we can get over this someday.

"I heard he's going back to the club," she says out of nowhere.

I pull her back in surprise. "You guys talked about it?"

"No. Kamii told me."

My eyebrows pull together in question.

"I guess I've never told you about Kamii, have I?" She laughs, leaving me even more lost. "Let's just say I was at the club as more than just a member."

"Huh? How?"

"Well…the owner of the club is my boss."

"What?" I cough out in disbelief.

"Yup. Believe me, I was just as shocked as you were when she told me. They asked me to join when she had a baby to be the secretive eye on the inside."

"So wait, you worked there?"

"Well, I mean, not worked but just kept an eye out on things."

"And you kept your eye on me, didn't you?" I pull her into me again, kissing her neck.

"Not as much as you kept an eye on me," she teases.

"You got that right. You were so hot."

I push my body into hers, hoping she gets where I'm going, the growing urge coming on strong.

"Do you miss it?" she asks, catching me off guard. "I mean, we are still members. We could go—"

I interrupt her with my mouth pressing wildly to hers. "Fuck yes, we could. Knowing that you're finally mine, at the club. Damn, Evangeline."

I kiss her harshly, pushing her up against the wall, having a hard time keeping my elation at bay.

She laughs at my sudden attack. "Well, glad we've had this talk then."

I grab my mask off the table and lean in to kiss her, "I love you," I whisper.

"I know," she deadpans back, laughing before saying, "I love you, too."

As we enter Club Bridge, I see Cole standing by the bar talking to a female, but his attention snaps in our direction when he sees us walk in. The uncertainty in his body language is a dead giveaway that he's just as nervous to see us. I offer a smile and when he smiles back, his shoulders loosen slightly, allowing mine to do the same.

I grab her hand and lead her to Cole, making sure he knows I'm okay with this. Once we're all standing next to each other, I look in her direction and let her take the lead.

"Hey there, handsome," she says, smiling. "This is Warroad, and I'm Warroadess. Good to see you tonight. Can we buy you a drink?"

Cole holds his hand out to me in a small peace offering. We shake and nod, knowing not much else needs to be said.

He holds up his drink. "I'm good, but I appreciate the offer."

I look at the girl he's already lined up for the night and slap his back. "Have fun tonight, bro."

He smiles, looking between Evangeline and me. "You guys, too."

The girl pulls on his shirt and he leaves with a shit-eating grin on his face. I lean down, placing my lips on Evangeline's neck, even more excited to get our evening started, together at last.

Chapter 40

EVANGELINE

"You ready?" I say, reaching over to hold Carter's hand before we get out of the car.

Our eyes meet, and both of us smile, taking a deep breath as we open our doors and begin our journey to the front door of a beautiful winery that we've been sitting in front of for the past few minutes.

His hand reaches for mine the second we're close together. I can tell he's nervous and just seeing him like this makes my heart soar even more for this man.

We contacted Benjamin's adoptive parents, and they were excited to have us come meet them, especially Carter. I heard a slight gasp when they heard his name, but I'm thankful they never asked questions, only focusing on all the joy we were able to bring into their lives and how amazing he is doing.

The day was set for us to come out to the winery, but they said they wanted it to be a surprise for Benjamin. He knows he was adopted, and they said he's talked about hopefully one day meeting his parents, especially his dad, so he'd have a clue about how big he'll be one day.

He's started playing baseball, and we're told he's pretty good. I know Carter played when he was Little League age, so apparently the apple didn't fall far from the tree.

We hear the sound of a wooden bat slamming against a ball reverberate against the hills around us, and Carter's face beams with his proud smile. "That must be him."

"Benjamin, I've told you, you can't hit the balls into the vineyard like that," we hear a woman call out.

"But, Mom, it's perfect. I have all the room in the world out here."

"Yeah, but how are you going to go find that ball you just hit?"

"It was an old one. I don't need it back."

She laughs. "Not the point, son."

We both chuckle to ourselves as Carter knocks on the door.

Not long after, the door swings open, and the woman I remember from ten years ago smiles brightly back at me. "Angie," she says, holding out her arms wide to me.

"Susan, it's great to see you again."

"You have no idea how great it is to see you, my dear. So this must be Carter."

He reaches his hand out to greet her. "Yes, it's nice to meet you."

"My, my, Benjamin looks just like you. My God," she says, placing her hand over her chest and stepping back to admire Carter for a second. "Here, come in. Roger," she calls out. "They're here."

A man steps from the kitchen with a welcoming expression on his face. "Angie, how are you?"

His arms reach around me in a hug like we've known each other for years. I clear my throat, letting them know. "I've actually decided to change my name back to my birth name, Evangeline."

I smile, looking over at Carter, and he grips my hand, giving me support.

"What a beautiful name, sweetheart, good to know. Now let me introduce you to someone just as beautiful as the two of you."

They open the back doors of their home, revealing a picturesque view that millions would die for. For acres and acres, all you see are rolling hills of vineyards with more of the same lining the backdrop. But right in the middle, up front stands a young boy throwing a ball high in the air and catching it with his glove.

"Benjamin, there's someone I'd like you to meet," Susan announces.

He turns to us, and instantly my eyes fill with tears. She was right. He's the spitting image of Carter. I turn to look at Carter, and the smile on his face says it all.

"Throw me one," Carter yells out, letting go of my hand and stepping in front of everyone.

Benjamin turns toward us and without missing a beat, throws the ball right to Carter, who catches it and throws it right back.

"Nice one. What position do you play?" Carter asks.

"League rules say we have to switch around positions but mainly first and pitcher. Do you play?"

"I like to hit the batting cages whenever I can."

"Benjamin," Susan yells out, "come here."

After throwing the ball one more time to Carter, he jogs the rest of the way to us.

"Honey, I have some people I want to introduce you to." She pauses, looking over at us.

Carter joins me again, holding my hand as we both anticipate his reaction.

"Benjamin, I'd like for you to meet your birth parents, Evangeline and Carter."

"Carter? That's my middle name," he says, surprised.

We all chuckle as we wipe the wetness from our eyes. "Yes, it is, bud," Susan replies.

Benjamin slowly walks our way, looking at Carter and then at me. "You're tall," he announces to Carter, making us all laugh again.

Susan speaks up, "He's the tallest in his class, and he always wondered who he got it from and how tall he will be. It's an obsession of his."

"Yes, I'm six-three," Carter says with pride.

"Did you hear that, Mom? Six-three. I'm going to be huge!"

The laughter that fills the area is contagious. Leave it to a little boy to break the tension or the anticipation of a scary moment and make it like it's nothing more than figuring out how tall he'll be one day.

Epilogue

EVANGELINE

"It's time," I announce, standing in the doorway of our bedroom.

It's been a year since we officially started dating again, and I've loved every minute. I didn't know life could be so good having that special someone around since I've lived so long on my own, but now that I have someone to share my life with I'll never be able to go back.

Carter reached out to Cole the other day, missing their friendship, and I was happy to see Cole was open to at least go to the batting cages like they used to. Hopefully, that friendship is on the mend.

We've also gotten to know Benjamin even more and have given his parents a date night out every once in a while so we can take him to the movies or out to a ball game. Sometimes I get sad thinking of what our lives would have been, but then I push it away, knowing our lives are exactly how they should be.

Especially now as I go into labor with our daughter.

"Now, like right now?" Carter jumps up frantically.

His anxiety cracks me up, especially for someone who's in the medical field.

He grabs my bag, and we head to the car. I've been feeling some pain off and on for a while now, but with this being my second baby, I knew I had time, so I didn't worry Carter.

Closing my eyes, I breathe in through my nose and out my mouth when I feel Carter's hand wrap around mine. Having him by my side for this birth makes tears roll down my face.

I can't believe how far we've come, and the full circle we've created. He lifts my hand to kiss the engagement ring on my finger then turns my hand over to kiss my wrist, where I got the same infinity tattoo through my line.

After he drops my hand, he grabs his phone and calls Benjamin's parents on the Bluetooth through the car.

"Carter?" Susan says excitedly, knowing why he's calling.

"It's time," he sings in the phone. "We're heading to the hospital now."

I laugh at her scream of joy. "Okay, we'll go get Ben from school. See you soon."

I smile, loving the idea of Benjamin being there with us. He was super excited to hear he's going to be a big brother.

This labor was different than my first. With Benjamin, I was in labor for fifteen hours, but our baby girl came in only four. The best part was having Carter by my side.

A couple of times I had to laugh at his demeanor and demands to make sure I'm okay by every nurse who walked in our room.

He was there, though, holding my hand the entire way and kissing my lips when the pain subsided. The support he gave me was more than any girl could dream of, and the look on his face when he saw his baby girl for the first time was priceless.

There's a swift knock on the door, and quickly Benjamin walks in without waiting for us to respond.

"She's here?" he practically yells as he approaches my bed with excitement.

Carter and I both laugh as I reply, "Benjamin, I'd like for you to meet your baby sister, April."

"You named her after a month?" he asks.

Carter lets out a loud laugh. "Yup. That's the month that changed my life forever." He leans down to kiss my forehead.

When I think about how far we've come, how much we've been through yet here we are, all together. I look up at Susan and Roger, who are standing in the doorway and mouth *thank you* to them.

Roger wraps his arm around Susan and pulls her closer as she holds her hand up to her mouth with tears rolling down her face.

"Can I hold her?" Benjamin asks.

We sit him down, and Carter picks April up, gently placing her in his arms.

There it is, my life is complete.

BLACK WIDOW

Preston

I bury my pain in a sex club. I can be anonymous and still be faithful to my deceased wife's memory. At the club, I can give and receive pleasure without guilt or attachment. My mask hides the lies of my past.

Kamii

My marriage ended tragically. Since then, the only excitement in my lonely, pathetic, workaholic life is reading erotic novels. However, I now have the chance to be whoever I want to be, where no one knows my past and will never be my future.

When their worlds collide, fantasies become a reality by pushing boundaries. The anonymity of Bridge offers protection from painful pasts, cunning schemes and dangerous lies. But when the masks are removed, there are no safewords to protect hearts and lives from buried truths.

GRAVITY

Gravity is not your normal, sweet romance of childhood friends to lovers. Spanning over twenty years—it's raw, it's real, asking the question if soul mates really exist.

Lily
At eight years old, the boy next door changed my life. He was the force pulling me toward him despite our differences. It was like magic.
We understood each other, supported each other and in the process became everything to each other.
But in chasing Trevin's dream, I lost myself along the way.

Trevin
Through tremendous heartache, she was there. Through fame and fortune, she was there. Loving Lily was the one thing I got right.
Eclipsing her in my shadow, I took from her until she was empty. Now I must do anything to prove I can be the man she wants, no, the man she deserves.

UNWRITTEN

Charlie Ashley, or Mr. Ashley as his clients know him, is a high-end male escort who gets paid thousands for whatever services his clients require. He's lived the last ten years alone, not letting anyone in, enjoying his success and provocative lifestyle.
Allison Hayes has no idea the man she is falling in love with is a male escort. She connects with Charlie through their love of music, playing a taunting game asking herself if she loves him, hates him or if she is going to save him.
After meeting Allison, Charlie enters a world where everything he knows no longer makes sense, leaving him too scared to move forward, yet making it impossible to look back.
But can he give up his entire life for love?

REWRITTEN

Charlie loves Allison more than life itself. But is his love strong enough to end a part of him?

Allison found the man of her dreams but fate keeps slapping them in the face with new challenges making her wonder if everything really does happen for a reason.

There are decisions to be made, relationships to mend and futures to be told all with one question; is their love strong enough to be rewritten?

*Rewritten is the conclusion of the Unwritten Series.

THE HIGH ROAD
(a novella originally published in *A Secret Affair* and releasing as a solo soon)

I walk through these halls with my tight bun, form-fitting uniform and a fake smile plastered across my face. My career is everything I've planned. I've made Captain in the Air Force and, even though I'm a female, I've gained the respect and recognition from my peers both below and above me. On the outside, I look like I've got it all, but on the inside, I'm slowing dying inside.

I never knew after one staggering night out, Alex would change my perception on life. He opened my eyes and gave me a glimpse into a world of what I was missing.

More of what I yearned for.

More of what I needed.

But he forgot to mention one thing… he is my subordinate.

Acknowledgments

After I wrote *Black Widow* readers started asking for another Club Bridge book. The thought never occurred to me to write another one, and it wasn't until my friend April Wells told me she wanted a book with a student and two teachers that the idea started rolling around in my head.

I knew that Angie from Black Widow would fit that roll and the two guys were introduced together already so the possibility was there. I just needed a song to guide me.

Music is my life and all of my books wrap around a song. One day I was delivering magazines with my "real" job and *Falling Inside the Black* by Skillet came on. As I listened to the song the entire book came to me, and *Falling Into The Black* was born. Though both guys weren't teachers, I was able to make at least one of them a teacher just for April.

When I started writing this I honestly had no idea who I wanted Evangeline to end up with so I wanted the story to decide for me. It wasn't until I was thinking about the cover that I remembered an amazing photo that my good friend, Lacy Pryde, had of her and her husband Josh. I knew then exactly who Evangeline and Carter were and that they would be together. Originally the photo was going to be on the front but I ended up moving it to the back cover after I found the photo that you see now.

A huge thank you to Stefanie Pace, Kelli Mummert, April Wells, Jeannine Colette, Cole Robitaille & Stacey Spence —notice where the name Cole Spence came from ;-) —, Stephie Walls and Chelle Lagoski Northcutt for being my beta readers and helping get Falling Into The Black to what it is today.

I've been lucky enough to work with Indie Solutions, Designed with Grace, Itsy Bitsy Book Bits and Wordsmith Publicity and I can't thank them all enough for their support.

With every book I release I love this indie world more and more. From the bottom of my heart, thank you to all of the blogs, readers and everyone who posts, leaves a review or tells a friend about my books. Thank you for making my hobby, with every late night, sore wrist and headache, worth it. Much love!

About the Author

Lauren Runow is the author of multiple Adult Contemporary Romance novels, some more dirty than others. When Lauren isn't writing, you'll find her listening to music, at her local CrossFit, reading, or at the baseball field with her boys. Her only vice is coffee, and she swears it makes her a better mom!

Lauren is a graduate from the Academy of Art in San Francisco and is the founder and co-owner of the community magazine she and her husband publish. She lives in Northern California with her husband and two sons.

She'd love to hear your comments and feedback. Please take the time to leave a review on Goodreads, Amazon, iBooks or wherever you purchased *Falling Into The Black*.

Sign up for her newsletter through her website at www.LaurenRunow. com to keep up to date about new releases.

Join her Facebook fan group at http://bit.ly/1UVmNeh

Follow her at:
www.facebook.com/laurenjrunow
www.instagram.com/lauren_runow
www.goodreads.com/author/show/14168280.Lauren_Runow
www.bookbub.com/authors/lauren-runow